BRIDE FOR THE SPACE COWBOY

MATCH MADE IN SPACE

PHOEBE BELLE

This is a work of fiction. Names, characters, businesses, places, events and incidents are either the products of the author's imagination or used in a fictitious manner. Any resemblance to actual persons, living or dead, or actual events is purely coincidental.

Copyright © 2024 Phoebe Belle

All rights reserved.

Cover design by Y'all That Graphic

No part of this book may be reproduced in any form or by any electronic or mechanical means, including information storage and retrieval systems, without written permission from the author, except for the use of brief quotations in a book review. Without in any way limiting the author's exclusive rights under copyright, any use of this publication (in any and all formats, including ebook, print, audio, translation, and any other formats) to "train" generative artificial intelligence (AI) technologies to generate text is expressly prohibited. The author reserves all rights to license uses of this work for generative AI training and development of machine learning language models.

❦ Created with Vellum

Chapter One
NADINE

"Come in," I say when I hear the knock on my door.

I live in a tiny apartment. Really tiny. It's all I could afford after I finally scraped up the nerve to leave my abusive boyfriend. He's rich, and he lives in the green zone. I don't care that he won't help me. This one-room apartment is a breath of fresh air compared to my life with him.

Maybe I have a shitty job and live in a cramped apartment, but I've never felt more free in my life. There's just that forever anxiety prickling down my spine that he's going to come back.

I open the door, and a sense of panic claws around my throat. I stare at him. "What are you doing here, Chad?"

My ex, who, objectively speaking, is handsome, narrows his eyes. "I thought you would come to your senses a little sooner," he says, brushing past me as he strides into my apartment.

He looks around the room with a sneer. It might be small, but it's cute. I have my own phone for the first time since I met him. Life on Earth may be a hot hellscape, but we still have technology. That's something.

I have a shelf on the wall where I keep my clothes. I'm standing in front of it beside the door. He moves so fast that I'm not prepared. He shoves me against the shelf, and the square metal edge digs in a line against my back. My breath is knocked out of my lungs for a moment.

I keep my wits and kick him in the balls as hard as I can. "Get out of here!"

Chad's groaning on the floor. I step around him, my pulse thundering through my body as panic and fear give me an unexpected surge of strength. I swing the door open and shove him out onto the dusty ground.

I grab my purse, relieved I already have my phone tucked into it. Racing through the door, I step around him and walk quickly away. I don't even feel the slightest twinge of guilt.

I'm so tired of Chad and his family. At this point, I'll hide from them if I have to. As I walk down the sidewalk with the sand blowing around me, my eyes land on a little flyer sharing an announcement about an opportunity for women to move to a new planet. I don't hesitate and start walking to the address listed. I have less than nothing to lose.

When I see the line gathered outside the office building, I pause and glance around. Aside from showing up for work and trying not to bake in the boiling-hot sun, there aren't many crowds on Earth. Not these days.

I hesitate before I see the sign. *Princess Jane invites you to Aphroditea. Let's face it, life is hell on earth these days if you're a woman. Come join us on a new planet. We need women. Bonus: women are revered on our planet. Hop in line, and you can learn all about it.*

I have zero reasons not to take this chance. I stand in the line, fidgeting with my purse strap and wondering if anyone will care that I have a black eye.

Murmurs spread among the waiting women, wondering if this Princess Jane is some kind of joke. Although, if you read our news online and in the old magazines that we occasionally find, there's tons of news about royalty on Earth.

It's not all sturm and drang here. We have a lively world on our internet, which somehow runs despite the scarce power. What little power there is generates from the green zone.

Eventually, I make it inside the building. I'm interviewed by the alleged Princess Jane herself. She even has a name tag that says so.

Jane runs through an explanation, sharing that Aphroditea has had humans living there for centuries. Apparently, cowboys from back in the day from both the United States and France traveled there. They even have creatures similar to horses. "I know it sounds wild," she adds with a smile. "They have mated with humans for centuries, like many other planets."

"Except Earth," I offer dryly. "Because we're dumbasses, and we've been busy destroying our own planet."

Jane rolls her eyes as she nods.

"So why do they need women there?" I ask.

"They host an annual festival to honor women. Two years ago, a storm struck the area during the festival, and many women died."

"Are the men human?"

"There are some human men there, but those that have descended from the space cowboys—"

"Are they really space cowboys?" I prompt with a sly grin. I like Jane enough to feel comfortable cracking a joke.

Jane flushes as she smiles. "Yes, they are. They are human-like but not entirely human," she explains. "Since they've mated with humans for years, we are very similar. Their skin is more bronze, and some of them have tails, but not all of them. I'll be honest, though, the tails are sexy," she says with an enthusiastic nod.

Jane seems familiar to me, but I can't place why. I'm pretty sure I've seen her before. When she's finished explaining this whole, honestly, wild situation, I say, "You seem familiar to me. Do I know you?"

She shrugs. "I'm not sure. I've only been away from Earth for a little while. About a month ago, I saw the online ad for a princess. I was tipsy when I was reading it and applied." She pauses, her eyes going wide. "Now, I'm actually a princess there."

"No joke?" I ask, almost dumbfounded.

"No joke. Trust me, I thought it had to be a joke too."

"Where did you work when you were here?"

"At one of the offices in the main factory."

We have three factories in town, one of which is the largest. We make products for the green zone. I work in one of the smaller ones. I'm also a fighter, but that's a whole other story.

"Wait a second," I say. "Were you engaged to Kyle Smith?"

Jane lets out a sigh. "I sure was. My not-so-best friend screwed around with him. Because she really wanted to go to the green zone." Her lips twist. "I thought I was going to get to go. Even though that whole thing sucked, I'm glad it happened. If I hadn't caught them, I wouldn't have applied to leave the planet, but trust me, life is so much better there. Do you have family or anything? Because that would be an issue. We don't want anyone leaving family or children behind."

I shake my head, my heart twisting. "Nope. My parents died. It's just me. And my ex-boyfriend beats me."

Jane's eyes narrow. "Well, then, I think you're perfect for this."

"When does this happen?" I ask, experiencing a surge of relief followed by anxiety.

"Today. Do you need anything from your apartment?"

I shake my head quickly. "Nothing at all. I can leave from here." Relief washes through me, and tears sting my eyes.

Jane reaches out and clasps one of my hands in hers. Her comforting touch is grounding. "I promise. This will be a better life."

Just then, the hairs on the back of my neck rise, and a prickle of awareness sizzles up my spine. I'm instantly drawn to look toward a door opening on the side of this large room. There are several tables where other women are being interviewed. A man enters, tall and imposing, his presence feels as if it fills the space.

I know instantly that he's not from here. His eyes narrow as his head whips around, his gaze locking with mine from across the room.

It literally feels as if a flame leaps through the air between us, leaving a wake of sparks across the room.

My pulse is pounding, and my breath becomes short. I've never felt anything like this.

Flustered and unsettled, I glance back toward Jane. "Who is that?"

Her eyes are warm. "He's second in command to Prince Asher. There's this thing..." She considers her words. "Their people believe in a true mate, but they don't all find one. They call the connection an infinity pulse. When I met Asher, it was the most intense thing I've ever experienced. Maybe that's what you're experiencing."

While I'm trying to absorb that crazy idea, the man in question walks straight over to me. His bronzed skin is almost shimmering. He looks at Jane and nods. "Your Princess."

I almost burst out laughing at that. Kayden's golden eyes hold mine, and I cannot look away. He studies me before reaching for my hand. "Follow me," he says.

I'm pretty sure I'd walk through fire for this man. I put my hand in his and stand. "Can I go with him?" I belatedly look back at Jane.

She smiles, waving us away. "Please go." She glances at Kayden. "Be nice."

I follow this imposing man who I know is not quite human. I'm drawn to him as though a magnetic force connects us. I don't understand it. I hope the bruising on my cheek isn't too bad. I'm tired, and I want to be anywhere but here. Well, not specifically here at this moment, but here on Earth. This could be my chance to truly escape.

After we walk through a doorway, he stops. I glance around

the narrow hallway before my eyes lock with his. He studies me. Under the harsh glow of the fluorescent lights, his skin shimmers. It's deep bronze and almost looks woven with a shiny substance. I'm nervous. I shift on my feet, and my fingertips tingle. I want to lift a hand and stroke his skin.

"What is it?" I finally blurt out.

His tiger-like eyes coast over my face. My belly feels ticklish and tingly.

"What happened?" he asks.

Even though he doesn't specify, I know he is asking about my bruised cheek. I take a shaky breath and will my heartbeat to slow its pounding.

"Someone hit me," I finally say. It's the truth without being too specific. I don't want to explain the whole story, and I hope he doesn't ask.

"I understand men don't treat women very well here," he replies.

His voice is low and rough on the edges. It sends sparks scattering through me, and my belly swoops. I take another unsteady breath as I nod. It's not a secret that women are practically second-class citizens on Earth.

The man tips his head to the side. "Who hit you?" he asks.

My chest and throat feel tight. Just talking about it brings up the fear I've lived with for too long. "My ex. I'm leaving. That's why I applied for this." Curiosity rises in the wake of my anxiety. "Are you called men on your planet?"

He nods. "You will come to our planet. No one will hurt you."

"How can you be so sure?" I press.

"We revere women. I will keep you safe."

Emotion rises swiftly inside, startling me. It's a mix of relief and gratitude and an almost-stinging sense of belonging. I don't really understand it.

I don't realize I'm crying until this man, whose name I don't even know yet, takes a step closer and lifts his hand to palm my cheek. His eyes on mine, he swipes his thumb across my cheek, catching the tear rolling down.

"I will keep you safe," he repeats.

I nod, whispering, "Okay."

My heart pounds so hard I can feel its echoing drumroll through my entire body. I'm filled with a sensation I don't recognize. An undercurrent of desire is threaded within it, but more than that is the intense sense of connection.

"I don't know your name," I blurt out.

"Kayden," he says simply. "And yours?"

"Nadine," I whisper just before he takes another step closer.

It's like a magnetic force field surrounds us. I can feel the heat emanating from his body. I'm startled to yearn for his lips on mine. It's as if we're speaking silently to each other.

Yes.

I hear his voice in my head as he steps closer, leaning down. There is some distance for him to lean. I'm short, and he utterly dwarfs me with his height.

I don't realize I'm holding my breath until I feel the brush of his lips over mine and let it out in a soft shudder. He angles his head to the side and claims my mouth.

His kiss is commanding and gentle. His tongue teases in to glide sensually against mine, so briefly that I let out a protest in whimper when he lifts his head. It's not enough. It's the very definition of a tease.

I'm bereft when his hand slides away from my cheek, his fingertips brushing lightly across the sensitive skin of my neck. I want to yank him back to me. I don't even recognize this part of myself. I clapped eyes on this alien man mere moments ago, yet I feel as if I know him on an elemental level.

"I must go," he says. "I will take you to Jane. She will take care of you."

I follow as he reaches for my hand and leads me back into the room filled with women applying to leave Earth. He leads me to Jane.

"Nadine will come to Earth," Kayden says.

He releases my hand, coaxing me forward where his other hand rests just above the dip at my waist.

Jane smiles at me. "Excellent."

I watch as Kayden walks away, my eyes lingering on his broad shoulders. Only then do I notice he has a tail.

Chapter Two

KAYDEN

A few days later

I resist the powerful urge to look over toward Nadine. She's standing beside Jane, our people's new princess. Jane smiles while she talks to her. Nadine brushes her hair back from her shoulder, turning to look around. The light briefly illuminates the bruising around her eye. Anger slices through me like a blade, the heat of the emotion cooling to an intense protectiveness.

When I watched Asher, my best friend since childhood, fall for Jane, I'd mentally scoffed. Not because I don't believe the infinity pulse is real, but because I thought he and I were too cynical for it.

Both of us have parents who were deeply in love. Even though the infinity pulse exists for our people, not everyone finds it. I assume I won't. Maybe because I'm bitter. Even though my parents had it, it had all fallen apart when my mother died in a raid. My father still pines for her, and I don't want to lose a love like that.

Asher stops beside me, cuffing me lightly on the shoulder.

When I slide my gaze sideways to meet his, his eyes are twinkling.

"What?" I prompt.

"Jane thinks you are meant for Nadine."

"I like Nadine," I reply, striving to keep my tone dry.

"Helena saw you kiss her," Asher adds, waggling his brows.

"Oh, for fuck's sake," I mutter as I lift a hand and run it through my hair.

"She thinks there is a pulse," he adds.

"Of course, there's a pulse," I counter. "My heart is beating, just like yours."

My old friend studies me for a moment as his gaze sobers. I'm hedging, and he knows it.

Infinity pulse is what our people call the connection, the very bond that links true mates. I never expected to feel it and even hoped I wouldn't be one of those who did.

I know Asher once thought the same. We'd joked for years about not worrying about being foolish.

"You don't always get to choose, my friend," he finally says.

I'm sworn to protect Asher. My family has served his family for generations, and loyalty is part of our nature. We are a protective people. That is how our planet has stayed strong, and we have taken care of each other. I'm Asher's primary bodyguard, just as my father has done so for Asher's father.

"I know I can't control everything," I finally say. "It's just—" I glance away and run my hand through my hair again. "My father still mourns my mother."

"Do you think your father would choose otherwise, after what he shared with your mother?" Asher asks, his tone almost soothing.

I finally glance back at him as I take a slow breath. "You know he wouldn't." Although I want to lie, I can't. Asher knows me too well.

"I can't change my infinity pulse with Jane and wouldn't choose to. I will fight for her again if I must." Our leadership has been facing an uprising from a town on the other side of our planet, a group of purists resistant to mating with humans even though we descend from them. They kidnapped Jane recently, and Asher fought with our elite fighters to rescue her.

"We'll see," I finally say. "It could be lust. It might not be a true pulse."

My friend's gaze turns knowing as he studies me for a few beats. "Fair enough. Maybe not. It's worth it if it is."

I let out a sharp breath, rolling my eyes slightly. "Point taken."

Just as Asher opens his mouth to say something else, Jane approaches, his princess, the very woman who'd stolen his heart in a matter of minutes. He holds her gaze. "My love," he murmurs.

Jane stops beside him, smiling between us before he catches her hand in his and laces his fingers with hers. "Yes?" he prompts.

"I was coming over to tell Kayden that we have an event this evening," she replies, her gaze shifting toward me.

"For what?" I ask.

"Matches," she says. "Nadine will be there if you are considering something."

I bite back a frustrated sigh. "Considering something?"

Jane, who I've only known for a short time, waggles her brows. "I may be new to Aphroditea, but I know about things."

"What things?" I nearly growl.

"Helena told me about the kiss," she says archly.

"Of course, she did," I mutter.

"I do understand you're known for being uncommitted, but..." Jane shrugs.

"But what?" I can't stop myself from pressing.

"You know how important this is. That storm killed so many women on Aphroditea. Without mating with humans, our people will be lost," Jane points out.

Despite how new she is to our planet, I feel a rush of pride that our princess has embraced her role as one of the leaders and protectors of our people and planet. Our people worship women as we should. They make life, and they raise us. Without them, none of us exist. For centuries, we've had an annual festival in honor of women. When a space storm blew in during the festival a few years ago, it killed so many women. We have reeled since then. In response, our leadership hatched a formal plan to recruit women from Earth to mate. Our people have mated with humans for centuries, from when cowboys from the United States West and France traveled here. It's strengthened both of our people. It's continued since then, yet we never had a formal plan to recruit mates. We never needed one, yet now, we are desperate.

"I know," I reply, nodding solemnly.

"I think things have been rough for Nadine on Earth," Jane adds. "She deserves a man who will protect her."

I know I have a problem when my heart twists sharply in my chest. I recall the bruising around Nadine's eye. I know things aren't easy on Earth for any woman. They're often treated terribly and abused. It's a good thing I don't live on Earth, or I would track down the man who hurt Nadine and make him regret ever touching her.

Although I don't worry about men on my planet harming her, the moment I contemplate the mere idea of her being with someone else, my fate is sealed. I glanced toward Nadine. As if she can feel the heat of my gaze from across the room, her head turns slowly, and her eyes snag mine. Even from a distance, I can feel the pulse, that draw to her as if heat and electricity vibrate through the air between us.

I force my eyes away only to find Asher and Jane studying me. Jane's gaze is knowing, and Asher's is laced with an understanding.

I let out a resigned sigh. "I would like to speak with Nadine privately. Can you arrange that?"

Jane nods. "Of course."

Chapter Three
NADINE

Anxiety spins in my belly, spiraling upward to tighten in my chest. My eyes keep darting over toward where Kayden stands with Jane.

Princess Jane. She's a freaking princess! You have to call her that.

Even though Jane has told us we don't have to stand on ceremony and call her by her title, I'm so fearful of losing my chance to stay here. I don't want to mess up.

I shouldn't have let Kayden kiss me. Because now I can't forget it. I should be preparing myself to meet someone else. So far, I'm a little bit blown away by this planet. It's beautiful, and it's not boiling hot like it is on Earth. Outside on Earth, I used to feel like an egg baking in the sun. People do actually bake eggs in the sun. It's a delicacy there because eggs are so rare. On Aphroditea, the environment is more temperate. The air is soft with a touch of humidity. There are trees and flowers and lakes.

For my entire life, they've been working on making Earth pretty again. They tell us that it will take centuries for the planet to recover from its nearly destroyed environment.

I shake my head. I need to stop thinking about Earth. That's my past. *This* is my new life. I don't ever have to travel back there again. Even if I don't get married off to someone who kisses like Kayden, they truly do seem to revere women here. No matter what, my life will be better. If I can just be safe from the man abusing me, that's more than enough.

I tear my eyes away from Kayden, trying not to linger on his broad shoulders and to wonder about his tail. Most of the men here have them.

Jane's assistant, Helena, has politely explained that some women also have them, but not as many. Helena has a pretty tail with hints of pink. The women here are taller and have the same shimmery skin as the men. However, their hue is silver rather than bronze. Helena has also explained this planet is a central hub for transportation all over the galaxy and that we will see many other alien people. I've already seen other beings, including a female orc. She was startlingly tall and intimidating at a glance but very friendly.

I twist my fingers together nervously, telling myself this will be okay. I have a safe place to live. I never have to see my abusive ex again.

I nearly jump out of my skin when I feel a light tap on my shoulder. My palm flies to my chest. I glance over to see Jane with her warm smile.

I let out a quick breath. "Sorry. I'm just a little nervous."

Jane nods. "Of course. It's a lot to come to a new planet. Ask me how I know?" she teases lightly.

I take a steadying breath, shrugging sheepishly. "It is a lot to absorb. When are we going to meet"—I circle my hand in the air — "the men?"

"I promise we won't parade you around. This event is intended to be casual. I came over because Kayden would like to speak with you."

My heart lunges in my chest. "He would?"

"Yes. Would you like to speak with him?"

"Should I?" I squeak

"If you're not comfortable, you don't have to talk with him."

She paused, tipping her head to the side as she studies me. "Do you know what you want?"

"I have an idea, but I'm not totally sure." My voice is breathless.

Jane's gaze sobers. "Kayden wants to mate with you. Like I mentioned before, I believe you have what is called an infinity pulse with him. Asher has explained that Kayden may have some fears about it."

"Oh."

I think to myself that simply not getting beaten is more than I ever imagined before. I can handle any baggage that comes my way. Even though this concept of the infinity pulse is, well, alien to me, I think I know what Jane means on an instinctive level.

"Will we be able to talk privately?" I ask.

"Of course. Follow me." Jane turns, sliding her hand through my elbow and squeezing gently. She walks me over toward where Kayden is speaking with Asher—Prince Asher to be specific.

Although the prince and princess, along with the king and queen are spoken of breathily, no one seems to bow or curtsy for them. When we reach them, Jane releases my elbow, saying to Kayden, "She's all yours." She gestures to a doorway just beyond us.

My heart pounds so hard that I can't hardly hear over the rush of blood in my ears. Kayden's golden gaze sweeps over me as he reaches for my hand.

Chapter Four

KAYDEN

Nadine's small hand is warm in mine as I lead her down the hallway and through a doorway. I turn to close the door behind me. The latch clicking is loud in the small room.

Before I even turn to face Nadine fully, I can feel the reverberation from her presence in my own body. It's like an echoing pull, drawing me toward her. The connection between us is powerful.

I take a breath to steady myself, squaring my shoulders as I face her. I'm not accustomed to this feeling. It's a sense of vulnerability, of being in thrall to this woman.

She's quiet as she waits. Her cheeks are flushed, and I can sense her nervousness. My eyes dip down, and I notice her fingers are laced together and one thumb rubs the other. She swallows, and the sound is audible in the space.

This room is unremarkable. Four square walls, the color white. It's an office. I've been in here before. When I was a boy, they used to have summer activities in this building for the children when we had our lessons. Now, the space is used for various community events.

The room's simplicity is a contrast to the connection vibrating between Nadine and me. I now understand why it's called an infinity pulse. Because it's a true pulse. Without knowing with scientific certainty, I believe her heart beats in tune with mine, an echoing drumbeat through my system.

She clears her throat, and my eyes lock to hers instantly. It feels as if electricity is snapping in the air, crackling and sending sparks in a shower around us.

"You wanted to speak with me privately?" she asks. She slides her tongue across her bottom lip.

The mere sight of her tongue is like a whip cracking through the air, sparking my arousal. My desire for her is like sky fire just before the clap of thunder, the air heavy and weighted.

I've traveled all over the galaxy. Every planet has storms, and every planet has something like thunder and lightning. Ours is most similar to Earth in terms of our environment and the way the storms work.

"Sky fire," I say, not intending to speak aloud.

"Sky fire?" she prompts.

"It's like lightning on Earth but a little different. It sizzles and makes a loud sound afterward. There are actual flames. That's why we call it sky fire," I explain.

"Oh. We get lots of lightning, but it almost never rains on Earth anymore. Do you get rain here?" she asks.

I nod. Without thinking, I'm stepping closer to her. The pulse is strong with a magnetic pull to it. I *must* be closer to her.

I stop just shy of touching her. Her eyes widen slightly, and her pupils dilate. I hear the sharp intake of her breath as her lips part slightly. "You haven't claimed me," she whispers. "So someone else may."

She lifts her chin a little, and I feel the dare. I also feel the uncertainty behind it and a sassiness that I love. She's annoyed with me.

"No one else will have you," I state.

"How do you know? What if I feel this way with someone else?" she volleys back to me.

. . .

I know logically that an infinity pulse can only exist once for anyone, and not everyone even experiences it. After years of watching my father grieve my mother and telling myself the infinity pulse isn't worth the potential pain, I can't even tolerate the mere idea that Nadine could be with someone else. A fierce sense of protectiveness surges inside me.

"That's not possible." I step closer, erasing the small distance separating us.

I can feel the warmth of her body and savor the way her cheeks flush deeper as she tips her head back to peer up at me. My tail twitches slightly, and my shaft lengthens and fills with need.

"Just like our princess said, you're all mine." My gruff whisper laces my words with the command rising inside me.

I can't hold back. I have to feel her lips underneath mine again. I slide an arm around her waist, coaxing her incrementally closer as I let it curve over her sweet bottom. She lets out this little "Oh!" when my arousal presses against the curve of her lower belly. I want her so very much. I can already feel my arousal leaking from the tip of my swollen cock.

I have experienced passion, need, want, and desire before, yet I've never experienced this need to claim a woman, to mark her. My eyes study her face for a moment, lingering on the faded bruising on her cheek. Thinking about who put it there sends a jolt of fierce anger through me.

Nadine blinks quickly, and I see pain flash in the depths of her gaze. An unfamiliar pain pierces my own heart. I feel as if I literally share her pain in my own heart. My hand tightens where it rests on her back.

"The bruising will fade," she says quickly.

"I will avenge you when I return to Earth," I vow.

Nadine shakes her head sharply. "No. I don't want you to do that. I want to leave my past behind me." I sense the steely strength underlying the pain she's experienced.

I force myself to take a breath. As much as I want to push the issue, I won't. It's her right. I would never try to control her that way.

"You'll be safe here," I say.

She swallows and blinks. "I hope so."

I've gone and gotten distracted from my very purpose. To kiss her, to assuage the need pounding like a fist inside, clamoring to be set loose to run wild.

I shift incrementally closer just as she places a palm on my chest. My heart lunges toward her touch as if it senses her claiming me.

"I don't want you to kiss me again if you're going to change your mind," she announces.

I study her for a long moment. "What do you mean?"

"You kissed me before, and you've ignored me since. Jane said you haven't spoken further about us since we were on the ship."

I cock my head to the side, realizing she doesn't know my history. Yet this connection between us tells her something about me.

I steady myself inside. "I'll explain more later, but I have my reasons for thinking I would never experience this." I gesture back and forth between us before placing my palm over hers, where it still rests on my heart.

Her hand turns, her fingers lacing with mine. I can feel the beat of her pulse against my palm.

"What is *this*? Infinity pulse?" she asks, her voice breathy and soft, sending tendrils of silk around my heart.

"Yes. Not everyone gets to experience it."

She studies me, her fingers tightening around mine as she squeezes gently. It almost feels as if she is trying to comfort me. This abused, bruised woman is trying to assure me my heart will be safe with her. She can and will bring me to my knees.

"I cannot deny it, so I won't. Someday, we will talk about it," I say.

She's quiet, and for a split second, I wonder if she'll deny me this kiss and all that it means.

As my fear begins to rise, she whispers, "Kiss me. We can talk later."

She leans toward me as I bend low to bring my mouth to hers. The initial touch is a brush, a scattering of sparks through the air. I hear the guttural groan rising inside me as I angle my mouth over hers, releasing her hand and palming her cheek as my fingers slide back to tangle in her hair and tilt her head to deepen our kiss.

It's everything I remembered and more. Touching her feels as if I've come home. There's a sense of rushing inside, water bursting forth, something breaking free inside me. The momentum of emotion and need spins faster and faster as I tumble into our kiss. I savor the way her tongue teases boldly against mine. My palm slides over the curve of her bottom as I pull her against me. I'm aching for her, down to my very bones.

The need drumming through me is unlike any I've ever experienced. It's primal and visceral. Yet there's a comfort in it as if we are spinning together in time.

Nadine makes a sweet, needy little sound in her throat, and I rock my hips against hers, desperate for her, desperate for more.

I want to luxuriate in her. I want time to slow and to absorb every increment of this kiss. Yet this competes with an overwhelming need to devour her. She tastes so good; she feels so good. It feels as if I've come home to a being rather than a place.

The need for air eventually forces me to lift my head. We stare at each other, our ragged breathing filling the room. Need beats the drum of my heart fiercely. I take an unsteady breath and scramble to find some control, but it keeps slipping. I cannot step away from her. I know I have to wait. When it comes to this infinity pulse, it's important to wait until after we are married to consummate.

I force myself to take a step back. I'm actually unsteady on my feet. That's how close I've come to losing control. Nadine stares up at me, her eyes wide and dark with passion.

"We will marry," I say.

"So..." She seems uncertain what she means to ask.

"In one week."

Her pretty eyes study mine. "You won't change your mind?"

I shake my head firmly. I've always known I must marry at some point. I thought perhaps after the storm that killed so many women on our planet that I would get a pass.

Now that I knew what it felt like to be with Nadine, no one else would do. I would either torture myself for the rest of my life or accept my fate.

"This isn't my planet," she says quietly and solemnly. "I have nowhere to go. You have to promise me."

"I always keep my word. I promise." I close the bit of distance between us. I have to kiss her again. I have to taste her again.

Everything is imbued with a deep intimacy twined within an intense arousal and passion that I've never experienced before.

I'm accustomed to feeling in control and like I can handle things. With Nadine, my control slips free instantly. Her tongue glides against mine, and she tastes so good and feels so soft. I hear the growl in my throat and the groan when her hand splays on my chest. I need more. Something to tide me over, something to carry me through the week until we can marry.

I nudge her back slightly until her hips bounce against a table that runs the length of the wall. I slide my hand down her thigh, reaching for her skirt. I fist it in my hand and drag it up. Her skin is soft and silky, and I cup my palm over her mound. She lets out this little whimper, a needy little cry.

I break free to stare into her dark eyes. "I need to touch you," I rasp.

Her audible swallow is like a lash of the whip, spurring me along. It's fuel poured on the fire of my desire, sending the flames licking higher and higher.

I tease my fingers over the silk covering her sweet pussy, gratified to find it wet. I hook a finger in the edge of her panties, pushing them out of the way as I delve my fingers into her slippery wet folds.

"Oh!" Nadine cries out.

Fuck me. Every sound she makes swells my cock even more.

I bury my fingers knuckle deep inside her. Her pussy clenches, and I watch as her breaths come in ragged gasps. Even though I didn't mean to take it this far, I must feel her come apart.

Her eyelids begin to drop. "Stay with me. Look at me," I say.

She drags her eyes open again, her gaze heavy and hot on mine. I pump my fingers, teasing my thumb over her swollen clit.

"I want to feel you come all over my fingers," I rasp.

She takes a shuddery breath, her hips rocking as I add a third finger, stretching her a little more. I feel her quickening, her breasts rising and falling rapidly.

"Now," I order as I swirl my thumb around her clit.

She cries out, her hips rocking to meet my touch. Her pussy tightens around my fingers. She shudders all over, and one of her palms slaps the table behind her.

My arousal is straining. It's all I can do not to yank my breeches open and lift her until I fill her with my seed. But I can't. I have to wait.

Her breath comes in ragged bursts. I keep my fingers inside her as I bend low to kiss her again. My tongue briefly tangles with hers before I lift my head.

"One week," I say.

I slowly withdraw my fingers and lift them to my mouth, tasting her nectar.

Chapter Five
NADINE

My brain is deprived of oxygen, and my lungs are barely able to do more than drag in small sips of air. My knees are liquid. I'm grateful for the table behind me and that Kayden stands strong in front of me. He still has one arm wrapped around my waist.

Even though I've just had the only climax I've ever had with a man—in this case, an alien man—my pussy clenches again at the filthy sight of him licking my arousal off his fingers. I have an ache in me that only he can fill. I want to be completely joined with him. The fusion of this connection has its own life.

Jane explained it, and Helene talked about it, but I didn't quite understand it. Even now, I feel like I'm grasping for something. It's ephemeral and almost otherworldly.

The sharp knock on the door startles me, snapping through this haze of passion and emotion. I take a shaky breath.

Kayden clearly hears it, but he doesn't move away. He seems unbothered by it as he lowers his hand. He reaches to smooth my skirt down over my waist again.

I scramble mentally, trying to gather my thoughts. "Will I see you before we marry?" I ask as he steps back. My eyes flick down to see the hard length of his shaft pressing against the leather of his breeches.

"Oh, yes. When there's this connection, we have to marry before we consummate fully. I will talk to Jane and Asher. Jane will help make the arrangements for our marriage. We will marry as soon as she says we can," he explains.

I study him for a few seconds before nodding. I knew from Jane that she had married the very day she landed on this planet. I'm wondering if things are different when you're not about to be a princess.

"Come in," he finally calls with a glance over his shoulder.

I feel disheveled—physically, emotionally, and mentally. I try to collect myself, but I can barely push away from the table. I remain leaning against it as the door opens. Jane peers into the room.

Her gaze bounces between us. "Well?" she asks.

"I'm claiming Nadine," Kayden says with a confident and clear tone.

Meanwhile, I'm still trying to absorb everything. Maybe it's the understatement of the century, but I'm on a new planet with an alien space cowboy. He's kissed me to utter distraction and made me come all over his fingers. Now, he's telling me I'm his, and we're going to marry soon. I'm just going with the flow.

Jane steps into the room. "Okay, I'll talk to Helena to start planning the wedding." Her eyes shift to me. "Are you comfortable with this?"

She looks at me as if I have some say. As a woman born and raised on Earth, I'm not accustomed to having *any* say. I shift uncertainly on my feet.

Kayden turns to hold my gaze. "On our planet, women can refuse any man claiming them. It's entirely your decision."

As if, I think to myself when he gives me a smoldering look before turning and departing the room.

He leaves me alone with Jane. She steps farther into the room and closes the door behind her. Her gaze travels over me. "Are you okay?" she asks.

Okay? I can't exactly tell her what just happened.

I swallow and nod. "Uh-huh."

"Do you want Kayden?"

"I do," I finally say. I can't imagine being with any other man.

She smiles. "Good. As you know, I'm still new here. I know from Helena that we need a little time to plan your wedding. It will happen next week."

"How come you didn't have to wait a week?" I ask. I can't believe it, but I want Kayden. Now. I want *all* of him as soon as possible.

Jane's lips twist to the side. "They had the wedding planned before I even got here. Asher went to Earth to find me. The whole princess thing was really important."

"Oh," I say. A week feels like forever, and I'm impatient. "Will I keep staying where I am now?"

"Yes."

Jane leads me out of the room. We pass by Kayden speaking with Asher in the hallway. I can feel the magnetic force when I walk past him. I turn to look, and his eyes hold mine. For the first time, I see him smile. His lips curl, just barely, when Jane says, "Nadine has agreed to be yours."

My belly flutters, and I think this might be the longest week of my life.

That evening, I'm back at the house I'm sharing with the other women from Earth. Aside from Jane, I'm the only one claimed. Considering that I experienced the most otherworldly connection of my life the very first time I clapped eyes on Kayden, I want everyone who came with us to find the same thing.

We're seated out in the courtyard with trees, flowers, and creatures like birds but a little different. This planet is what I imagined Earth was like before it got baked to a dry crisp.

A staff person pours us glasses of pink liquid. Jane smiles.

"Did you ever have a lemonade back on Earth?" she asks, her gaze encompassing all of us.

"Oh no. All I've ever had is water," Romi says.

"Water, and I suppose when I was a baby, I was breastfed," Melody offers dryly.

I like Melody with her sly sense of humor. She has bruising on her arm that looks like a handprint.

"Just water for me," I chime in. "My mom told me about lemonade. I hear they have it in the green zone."

"Ha!" Romi says, her brows hitching up. "The green zone. My parents were on the list to move there, but then they both died in the fire in the old factory."

"I'm so sorry," I say, reaching over and squeezing her shoulder. "I know what it feels like to be alone."

"Most women on Earth know that feeling well," Melody says softly.

Jane fills the silence that follows. "Anyone who comes here through my matchmaking service has no family left on Earth. That's part of the deal. Not because we want you to be alone. Helena explained that it's really important for you not to worry about who you left behind."

"Ohhhh," I say slowly. "That makes sense. Our bad luck on Earth can be good luck here."

Jane lifts one shoulder in a slight shrug. "I suppose. I don't know that there's any good luck these days for women on Earth. It's not as if things are perfect here either. I haven't had a chance to tell you what happened to me."

"What happened?" Romi prompts.

"You mean Aphroditea is not an idyllic oasis in space where nothing ever goes wrong?" Melody teases.

Jane takes a quick breath as she shakes her head. "It is beautiful here, and they do revere women, but it's not perfect. On the other side of the planet is another much smaller town. A faction has taken over leadership who oppose their people mating with humans. They kidnapped me."

We collectively gasp. "Oh no! What happened?" I ask.

"As you can see, I'm fine." She lifts both of her hands in the air, letting them fall. "Before I get into the scary part, have more lemonade."

I take a swallow, and the tart and sweet taste is unlike anything I could've even imagined.

"This is amazing!" I exclaim.

We take a few moments to savor it, but I'm impatient for more on what happened to Jane.

Jane jumps in, explaining, "They grow lemons here, but they were imported from Earth before they were gone. They have a garden program dedicated to cultivating plants from other planets, in addition to what is native."

"I heard about a seed storage place on Earth," Romi chimes in. "No one's ever found it, though."

"From what I understand, seeds started being transported here centuries ago. Asher knows the whole history. Earth is so bad, but it's not like that everywhere. They import and sell goods all over the galaxy," Jane explains.

I circle my hand in the air. "The kidnapping? You're kind of freaking me out."

"Oh, yes. I promise I'm fine. Asher had to get married and consummate his marriage officially." She rubs her hand over her belly. "As you can see, I'm expecting. While they are essentially a democracy here, their people believe in the lineage of their royal family. In each generation, the first heir, male or female, must mate by a certain age. Asher had not found a mate here on the planet, so he decided it was time for another expansion trip in the galaxy. Considering that Earth is so..."

She pauses, and we all chime in with descriptions, including unpleasant, miserable, awful, shitty, and more.

Jane nods in agreement. "All of the above. After so many women here died from the space storm during the women's festival, they decided to actively find mates on Earth. Humans have traveled here for centuries, so that's not new, but they formed a plan to expand their lineage with matchmaking. Asher had to marry quickly to prevent an uprising over the royal succession. The small group of men opposed to this in another town kidnapped me to try to prevent me from having Asher's baby with him. Asher and a team of fighters saved me within the first night. You needn't worry about your safety. New security measures are in place to protect everyone here. I feel safe," Jane says confidently.

"You have security," Romi points out.

"And isn't Kayden, Nadine's guy, one of Asher's bodyguards?" Melody asks.

Jane nods. "He is, but I'm safe. The opposition is much weaker now, and their plans are exposed. Since the dawn of time, I suppose, politics has been a problem all over the galaxy. This small group is currently in power in that town, but the people they're trying to rule over don't agree with them. Kidnapping me was a big mistake on their part. Asher says he hopes it's weakening what little influence they have."

"Do any of us need to worry about getting kidnapped?" Romi asks.

Jane shakes her head. "I don't think so. To be honest, that event for me was no worse than what I went through on Earth. There are kidnappings all the time there. Sure, there's a government"—Jane uses air quotes for this— "but it's every person for themselves. Women are second-class citizens there, literally. Here, they revere women. Mating among people from different planets—human, alien, and more—is widely accepted all across the galaxy. We would know all this if Earth wasn't so miserable to live on."

Melody nods vigorously. "Maybe it's a little disconcerting to learn that Jane was kidnapped, but it's no worse than anything I've already been through. My parents died in that fire, but before that, a man kidnapped my mother for several weeks. He was trying to steal her from my father because he didn't have a family. Women were practically slaves there, as far as taking care of things for men."

"I know!" Romi chimes in. "Just not being looked at like I'm nothing feels good here."

Melody glances at me. "What does it feel like with Kayden? We see Jane, or Princess Jane, with Prince Asher." She winks as she casts a teasing smile in Jan's direction. "But is it as intense as it looks? Those two look like they're about to start a fire when they're together."

Heat swirls inside at the mere thought of Kayden. "I don't know how to put it into words. It feels like attraction, but it's so much more."

As I ponder, Jane chimes in, "It's hard to explain. Until I experienced it with Asher, I would've thought the whole idea of the infinity pulse was ridiculous."

I nod vigorously in agreement. "Absolutely. It's much more than I ever imagined. Honestly, it feels so good to have someone treat me well and to feel safe." Abruptly, tears sting my eyes. When I swipe at my tears, I feel the lingering soreness from where Chad hit me.

Melody leans over, curling her arm around my shoulders and squeezing. "We all understand. We hope for the best, but the bar is so low on Earth that we could trip over it."

Jane's eyes catch mine. "Maybe we didn't go through the same things, but life on Earth isn't good. No matter what happens here, it will be better," she says softly.

Chapter Six
KAYDEN

Helena eyes me, hands on her hips with her sharp tail twitching. "This is how it has to be. You serve the royal family. Your wedding is important."

I bite back a sigh. "Fine," I grumble. "I just thought—"

Helena doesn't give me time to say anything else. "You know better. You thought you would never experience the infinity pulse, so you didn't plan on getting married."

I press my tongue into my cheek as I chuckle. "Just tell me what to do, then."

"That's my job," she says tartly.

Only three more days are left until my wedding. Every time I see Nadine, all I can think is that I can't wait any longer. Yet I'm waiting.

Someone swipes my tail as I walk out of Helena's office. I glance over my shoulder to see Asher leaving his office just behind me. He grins.

I turn to face him. "Yes?" I ask, my tone dry.

The list of people who tease me by swatting at my tail is short. It consists of Asher and a few of our friends among the group of families who protect and work directly for Asher's family.

"Based on the look on your face as you came out of Helena's office, I'm assuming she gave you a little lecture about how the wedding will be handled?" he teases as he falls into step beside me.

"Exactly. I presume you received the same information around yours?"

"In my case, Helena told me exactly how it would be before we even took the journey to Earth. I didn't have time to wait. Are you ready?" he prompts as we exit the hallway and enter the main entry area for this building.

This large building has many windows looking out over the royal city. We stop in front of the view. You can hear the hum of ships landing nearby in the docking area. A distinct blue haze blankets the mountains in the distance. The rising sun shimmers over the lake.

I love our planet and our town. "As ready as I'll ever be," I belatedly answer. I feel Asher's gaze and turn to face him.

"We have a meeting today with Honnell and the judicial council," he begins, referring to one of the men who've been making noise about the royal succession in another town. "I'd like you to come with me."

"Of course I'll be there."

That afternoon, we land on the other side of the planet. We walk into the meeting place in this town. Until the past few decades, things have been quiet, politically speaking, on our planet. Then a new family rose to power over here. They don't have the support of the majority in their area, but they are loud and pushy. They create the impression that they have more support among their people than they do.

They've been grappling to topple Asher's family from the royal leadership after they push their elected leaders out of power.

Since the scare with Jane, they've lost significant influence, and things are much more unstable here.

We wait outside. Asher leans close, his tone low. "We're only meeting to clarify the guidelines around the upcoming trials. Nothing more."

"Understood."

A few moments later, we are ushered in. The judicial chiefs oversee our entire planet. They meet in whatever town events occur.

Jane's kidnapping, in my opinion, was unforgivable and should have serious consequences. Yet it remains to be seen how they will handle it.

The town's leadership is seated. Things have been unsettled here ever since the kidnapping. Some want to have new elections in their town. Others are willing to wait and see what happens with the trials.

Once we are seated, I glance over. Asher's fists are curled tightly.

"You okay?" I murmur, sliding my eyes toward him.

He nods once.

Those who have been arrested for Jane's kidnapping are brought in. The next hour involves jostling over what evidence can be submitted. The uprising faction behaved as usual, loud and complaining. When our representatives finally speak, they outline our people's history of government, how our planet has been protected and led safely by Asher's family for centuries, and how we support democracy and the people's voice. They draw a contrast to the leadership in this town and how they are trying to destroy all of that.

We've already agreed that Asher will not speak to prevent his emotions from overtaking him. I've seen the infinity pulse before, but witnessing it with him is something else altogether. His feelings for Jane are intense and can override his usual calm state.

That said, I now understand how he feels. Nadine feathers along the edges of my thoughts most of the time.

One of the judges, a powerful woman, glances around. She quietly studies those who had orchestrated the plot to kidnap Jane and hold her until she gave birth.

"Regardless of the arguments about royalty and leadership, and whether there should be mating with other peoples, you harmed a woman, and our people have revered women since the inception of our planet. Bringing harm to a woman is your greatest crime. We have heard the evidence and will consider it, but in the meantime, you will remain held," she says, her tone clear and firm. "We cannot trust you not to try to harm women again. We also know our people have been mating with other races for centuries."

Quiet descends on the courtroom as the men are escorted away. Because of what this small group of people have done within this league, they have even fewer women for mates. Women are fleeing this area. No one wants to be a part of it. These men aren't savoring them and protecting women as they should.

I know the struggle will continue, though. The small group has a hold on some. Until we can break their hold, we will be dealing with their mess.

After we leave, Asher turns to me. "We must fix this."

I pause. "Fix what?" I think I know what he means, but I'm not sure.

"Repair the damage they've done. It isn't just them, but how they have poisoned others."

I study him for a long moment. "Understood, but it will not be easy."

When we leave, we encounter an elderly woman from this league. She gestures for us to come over to where she stands, waiting a ways outside the judicial building.

"Yes?" I say when we stop in front of her.

Asher is flanked by his team of guards. Although it would be unspeakable for someone to try anything here, I don't trust anyone.

"Your Prince," she says with a dip of her head.

Asher tips his head to the side. "Yes?"

"What is it?" I press.

She glances around before looking back at Asher. "All of those who are actively involved in the planning have been arrested," she says, keeping her voice barely above a whisper. "But you must know we are still concerned. Honnell's father, who started this whole mess, is still grumbling. He's stirring the pot, upsetting people with lies. I know you all have tried not to take over leadership in this league, but I think you need to get more involved. Without it, they're going to keep doing this."

After a long moment, Asher nods. "We appreciate your feedback, but we cannot interfere with the democratic process."

"You must ensure that they don't intimidate people regarding voting. That is how they won," she says. "We are ensuring that more women make their voices heard and that more women vote. They continue to try to intimidate and create problems. I think your people should come here more."

"We are your people," Asher clarified. "There is no separation."

Concern lingers in her eyes. "I know, but many have forgotten that."

After we depart, Asher is quiet on the transport home. When we land, I glance over. "Jane should travel there. She's not afraid. Her life on Earth has prepared her to deal with strife."

Asher considers me for a beat. "That's a very good point. All of the women from Earth are prepared for conflict. I imagine any of them would be happy to accompany Jane here."

"Nadine will." My voice is confident.

I know she will. She's fearless and bold.

Chapter Seven
NADINE

It's one day until the wedding, and I'm beyond impatient to see Kayden.

That morning, I dress and slip out early to stop by a café that I've discovered with Melody. I like many things on this planet, but I love the freedom to walk safely. On Earth, aside from the brutal heat, there's always the risk of walking alone and having some man looking for a mate try to kidnap you.

On Aphroditea, I feel safe and protected. I walk into the café, and a female orc, Trudy, smiles at me. She's startlingly tall. "Hi!" she says when I stop at the counter.

"Good morning. What do you recommend today?" I ask.

Jane has set me up with a tab here, explaining that the royal family will take care of me until I find a job.

Trudy grins. "You like the bitter coffee, but I think you should try one of the sweet ones."

"I'll try it! Everything you suggest has been great."

She quickly made me something that she called a froth latte, explaining the term came from Earth during an era when they made these. It's sweet and light, and I love the flavor.

"You know, you could get a job here," she says with a smile after she serves me.

"I could?"

"Yes. We have several open shifts because we're expanding. I know you're getting married, and that's a big deal, but this would be something you could do once you're settled. Maybe after your honeymoon, which I hear will be all kinds of fun," she teases.

My cheeks get hot. "Do you know what an infinity pulse is?" I ask.

Trudy nods. "I've heard about it. Orcs don't usually experience that, but it's all the rage here. Do you feel it with your man?"

Heat blazes through me as I nod.

"Kayden is one of the royal bodyguards. You will be important here once you marry him," she points out.

I can't help my nervous laugh. "I'm still getting used to the whole royal thing. It was in the old news on Earth, but that's it."

Trudy rolls her eyes. "I've been to Earth. Kind of sucks for people there these days." She shakes her head.

"Where else have you traveled?" I ask.

"Here, Earth, and my birth planet. That's it. Some orcs travel more than others. I actually like it here. It's kind of peaceful. Even though I'm not from this planet, it's nice to be somewhere where women are revered. It's a pretty cool place to live."

"I have to admit I'm not used to it," I reply.

She snorts, resting her hip on the counter. "Earth isn't the only place that treats women like shit. Trust me on that."

"Will you be at my wedding?" I ask.

"I got the invitation just the other day. Of course I'll be there. You're my new friend." Her eyes twinkle.

I smile. "I'm glad you'll be there." I lift my cup to take another sip just as a cluster of customers enters the café. "I'll see you there tomorrow. I understand I'll be busy between now and then."

Trudy waggles her brows. "You'll be *really* busy for the week after."

Her sly laughter follows me. With my cheeks burning up, I turn to leave. I've heard all about how Kayden and I will have our honeymoon in our own private home for an entire week immediately following the celebration after our wedding. I can't wait.

Chapter Eight
NADINE

Jane holds up a dress of navy silk. "What do you think?" she asks.

"I think it's beautiful."

Considering my options before arriving here—being forced to marry an abusive man—I don't care too much about what I wear for my wedding. I'm relieved to feel safe.

My ex's family had money and lots of it. Things had been so bad with him that I hadn't even wanted the opportunity to live in the green zone. I would've gladly taken living in the scorched, dry, dusty town where I worked in a dreary job over marriage to him in the green zone.

"Nadine?" Jane prompts.

I shake my thoughts out of the past and back to the present. I study her quietly. "You know, anything is better than what I would've had on Earth. The dress is gorgeous. Do you think it will fit?"

Her eyes crinkle at the corners with her smile. "We'll adjust it if needed."

"I'm not royalty like you," I tease.

She rolls her eyes. "You don't have to be royalty here to be treated well."

I try the dress on. The fabric is soft and silky against my skin, but the fit is a touch too tight. At Jane's direction, a friendly seamstress helps make a few adjustments.

Jane explains the upcoming ceremony and tells me that I will stay with Kayden for a full week afterward.

"Okay," I say, taking a quick breath in. "He mentioned that. But where is his home?"

"You'll share a new home with him."

"A whole week alone?" While I am very much looking forward to time along with Kayden, an entire week feels like a luxury.

Jane's smile is wide. "I promise you'll enjoy it."

My belly flutters. I'm so impatient to finally take this next step.

That afternoon, Jane walks with me over to where the ceremony will be held. "Here," she says, "Women give themselves away at their wedding. We have our own power and independence."

We walk through a large office area that I've been with her before we go down a covered walkway to another building. It's sort of like a church, but not really. It's beautiful, like so many of the buildings here. Modern and airy.

My heart races before we even enter the main room. Even though I feel safe here and the idea of going back to Earth elicits a sense of sadness and weariness, this is also new and different.

I'm on a new planet, and I'm about to pledge my heart to an alien space cowboy. It's definitely unlike anything I ever expected to do.

I take an unsteady breath as Jane leads me through a doorway, murmuring, "Wait here."

I have become close to the women I traveled here with. They're all waiting for me. Melody and Romi smile at me.

"Are you ready?" Melody asks, her voice soft.

I take an unsteady breath as I nod. "Ready as I'll ever be."

Melody's honey-blond hair gleams under the sunlight coming from above. The entire roof of this place is glass. Natural sunlight shines through, casting a warm glow throughout the space.

I still can't believe I'm the first one of us to be mated. What has happened with Kayden feels truly otherworldly.

Jane peers through the doorway again, gesturing for me to come with her. We walk down a short hallway into a large open space. Melody and Romi sit to the side near the front, where Jane gestures for them to go.

I follow her with my pulse drumming. Kayden waits at the front. My heart feels like it's going to crack my ribs. I can hardly breathe.

Kayden is dressed simply in his usual breeches with a navy silk shirt open at the collar. His bronze skin shimmers in the light coming through the glass above. His gaze snags mine, and I can't look away as I approach.

A moment later, I'm standing in front of him, and all I can see is him. Everything else fades away.

A tall woman leads the ceremony. Kayden pledges his heart, his protection, and his body to me. I repeat the vows back to him. I can feel the sizzle of electricity joining us as our pulses beat together.

His hands hold mine as the woman marrying us gestures above our hands, and light moves like an infinity symbol surrounding his wrists and mine.

I take an unsteady breath. I can feel the heat of the band of light joining us. I'm lost in his gaze when he bends low to kiss me, sealing our vows.

Time passes in a blur. The king and queen congratulate us on our marriage. Jane and Asher lead the procession out. While Kayden is usually one of the guards for Asher, he's not for today.

The royal procession surrounds us, and we walk outside along a path. It feels surreal to hear birds chirping and a gentle breeze blowing.

We walk up a sloping hill and through a flowered archway into a walled garden. Long tables are set up with food piled high. Kayden and I are seated at a table with Asher and Jane and the king and queen. The queen is very kind.

The food is incredible, but I feel Kayden's presence beside me the entire time. My brain is filled with static, a cacophony of the intensity of emotion and sensation of being close to Kayden, jumbled with the enormity of the event.

I'm married to an alien space cowboy. Mere weeks ago, I felt trapped on Earth.

Finally, the celebration winds down, and the crowd gradually breaks apart. Jane and Asher come over to walk us out.

Jane congratulates me and murmurs something, but I don't even register it. Somehow, I manage to be polite and say my goodbyes as we prepare to leave. Kayden's hand is warm around mine. Moments later, we walk outside down a street with flowers and trees flanking it.

I've walked through the town daily since I've been here on the planet. I take in the familiar sights as we pass through the main part of town. Kayden leads us down another street. Life carries on around us, with some people zooming around on those hovering transport vehicles and others walking. A soft breeze gusts through the air, and I savor the freshness.

"This way," Kayden says as we turn along the path. We walk through a flower-lined arch that leads us into another walled compound.

"Where are we?" I finally ask.

The small garden is beautiful, with more trees and flowers. I'm still adjusting to living somewhere that isn't just dry, baked dirt with dust blowing.

"This will be our home," he says.

I glance ahead to see a home that blends beautifully into a

hillside. It's low with a roof that angles up. Kayden leads me through the entryway, and I quickly take in the airy space. Light comes in through windows that run the length of the house.

This is the first time Kayden and I have been alone today. The day has been so full that I almost haven't been able to think. I take an unsteady breath and glance up at him as he turns to face me.

I'm instantly ensnared in his gaze. His golden eyes bore into mine.

I try to take a breath, but I can barely get any air. Heat blazes through me as my pulse rampages. "We're married!" I suddenly blurt out.

He studies me for a beat. "We are." He's still holding one of my hands, and he lifts his other hand, his fingers trailing through the ends of my hair where it falls over one of my shoulders. "How do you feel?"

"Good." My voice is breathless. I swallow nervously.

His lips quirk slightly at the corners. "It's been too long since we kissed."

My eyes lock onto his mouth. I manage a shaky breath as I nod.

He takes a step closer, and his palm lands on the side of my neck. His lips brush over mine once and then again. He pauses, lifting his head incrementally. When he speaks, his words are moving against my lips. "I don't think I can wait."

"I don't want you to wait." I'm trembling with need.

The heat of his body is like a force field surrounding me. My arm slides around his waist. Even though I know he has a tail, I'm a little startled when I feel the twitch of it. We are pressed together from head to toe.

Kayden fits his mouth over mine, his hand gripping my hair as he angles my head to the side. His kiss consumes me completely.

It's as if we are melting together, his tongue tangling sensually with mine, his kiss bold and masterful. All I want is him. All I want is more.

I shift on my feet as my need rapidly builds. His kiss kindles the fire inside me, the flames licking higher and higher.

We break apart, breathing raggedly and deeply. I look up at him, feeling nearly wild inside. My control has snapped.

He is the only thing that anchors me and keeps me from completely losing control. Kayden is the very source of my need and intense desire.

He lifts me in his strong embrace and carries me. I hear the echo of his footsteps on the floor as he strides quickly out of the entryway. My senses take in bits and pieces of our surroundings. The light streaming through a skylight. A room with a bed. He sets me down on the end of the bed, his palms resting on either side of my hips as he stares deep into my eyes.

"I want you. Now." His words are a gruff command.

I can't even speak as I stare at him and nod. I'm frantic and needy in a way I've never experienced. I tug at the buttons on his shirt. He's kissing me as he deftly unlaces my dress.

Cool air strikes my skin as my dress falls to my waist. His touch is warm. One palm slides down my side, and the other curves over my belly. My pussy clenches, my arousal soaking my panties.

His lips blaze a hot trail over my skin. He murmurs something against the hypersensitive skin of my breast just before I feel the hot shock of his lips closing around a needy, taut nipple. I arch into him, crying out as I feel the graze of his teeth.

A moment later, he releases it. His gaze burns into mine.

"Kayden..." I gasp.

I'm impatient, and I want so much, all of it, all at once. I'm yanking at the laces on his breeches as he shrugs out of his shirt. I take in the warm surface of his bronze skin that shimmers under the skylight above.

He's strong and fit. My palms trail over his muscled chest before my eyes dip down to where I see the hard ridge of his shaft. I need to see him; I need to touch him. His cock springs free a moment later. It's swollen and proud, his arousal glistening on the crown.

I can't help myself. I curl my palm around it, sliding my thumb over the tip and swiping his cum away. I lift my finger to taste him. He lets out a little growl when I lick it, tasting a salty flavor.

Chapter Nine
KAYDEN

I look down at Nadine. Her eyes are wide and dark with desire. There's a saucy glint in her gaze as she licks the tip of her thumb, tasting my seed.

Her cheeks flush a deep shade of pink. In the heat and intensity of this moment, I forget all of my reservations about allowing myself to give in to the infinity pulse that beats with its own heart between us.

She sits on the end of our bed. Her wedding dress has fallen to her waist, exposing her plump and full breasts. As I take her in, I see the fading bruise underneath her eye. It elicits a surge of protectiveness. I will make sure she's always safe. I will protect her with the shield of my very being, with the shield of our connection.

The mythology about our people includes stories about the infinity pulse casting a spell of protection for the couples blessed enough to experience it. Its rarity is alleged to give it more power.

I take a breath and lift a hand, trailing my knuckles along the side of her cheek and down, gratified at the feel of goose bumps rising on the surface of her skin in the wake of my touch. Her eyes hold mine, her breath coming in sharp pants, and her lips parted.

"Please don't make me wait," she whispers.

"As you wish," I nearly growl as I dip my head to kiss her again.

I consider myself a man in control of his impulses. I always have been before Nadine. With her, my control goes up in smoke, burned in the fire of our connection. She dissuades me of any notion of control. It isn't so much what she does. It's *her*. It feels as if every time we touch, the power of our link strengthens, vibrating through us.

Our kisses go on and on and on. But I need more; I want more. She tugs at my clothes. I lift her off the bed, and her dress falls in a puddle around her feet. I kick my clothes out of the way, and we are both bare. We stand still through several echoing beats of my heart. Time feels liquid here, with every second flowing into the next.

I lift her again, stretching her out on the bed. She makes these little sounds in her throat that drive into me like spurs, digging into the flanks of a desire already galloping. My raw need spins out of control, and I stretch out over her, my hands greedy. We continue to explore with our hands and teeth and tongues. Her skin is silky, soft and dewy with passion.

I'm begging as much as she is. *Please, more, now.*

I slide my hand over her belly, loving the soft curve of it. Pushing her thighs apart, I tease my fingers into her core. She's slick with her arousal. I have to taste her even though I'm impatient to be inside her. I need to carry her taste on my tongue when I bury myself inside her.

I dally with one nipple and then the other, savoring the sting on my scalp when she tugs at my hair and arches up against me. I make my way down her lush body in a trail of kisses.

I pause to take her in. Her pink pussy glistens, and her arousal is smeared on the insides of her thighs. I dip my head, bringing my mouth to her sex as I gently explore her folds with my tongue and suck lightly on her clit. Every little sound she makes sends another throb to my cock.

I need her to find her pleasure before I do. I sink two fingers into her, stretching and pumping. She's tight. Our people don't stand on the ceremony of virginity, but it's clear she's never been with someone like this. Her walls are tight and clenching around my fingers. She's crying out, and I feel her body quickening. Her hips buck roughly against my mouth when I swirl my tongue around her swollen and needy clit. Her keening cry is startled as her entire body trembles. I stay with her until she relaxes, and I give her a lingering kiss on the sweet curve of her belly as I rise above her again.

I ease my weight over her carefully, resting in the cradle of her hips. My thick crown notches at her entrance. She's still trembling, and I feel the kiss of her slick arousal tempting me to let go and plunge inside her roughly.

Her heavy-lidded eyes hold my gaze. Her hair is in a tousle on the pillows, framing her face. "Have you been with a man before?" I ask even though I know the answer.

"Not completely," she says. "I'm not afraid."

"I'll try to be gentle," I say, knowing this is painful for some women. I shift against her, nudging into her slippery, wet folds.

Her eyes stay locked with mine as I slide in slowly. She lets out a sharp breath when I feel myself pass through the tightest area. I hold still, easing forward until I'm fully seated inside her. I nearly come at the feel of her tight, rippling core around me.

She lets out a little sigh, and I feel her begin to relax. I rock forward subtly and then again.

Chapter Ten
NADINE

"Look at me," Kayden whispers.

I drag my eyes open to find his golden gaze waiting for me. I feel full, deliciously stretched with him inside me. The stinging burn of his initial entrance has faded, and I breathe slowly as my body adjusts to him.

Looking into his eyes helps me relax. This connection feels unbreakable, the power of it intense.

"How do you feel?" he asks, his voice gruff.

I take a moment to catalog the sensations dancing through my body. I'm still riding the endorphin high from the climax he gave me with his fingers and his mouth. Pleasure swirls in slow eddies through me. I love the way his weight feels on me. It's a reminder of how powerful he is. The contrast of his strong, muscled body against my soft curves is delicious. I feel held, almost protected in the shelter of being joined with him like this. I take a shuddery breath, replying, "I feel good."

He studies me. "Are you in pain?"

I take another breath. "I'm sensitive but not in pain."

I'm caught in his electric gaze as he searches my eyes. He lowers his head slowly, giving me a lingering kiss.

I think he means to comfort me, but I don't need that. My

body is restless, and I shift under him, rocking my hips toward his.

He lifts his head, shifting up on his elbows and lacing his fingers through mine. He rocks into me slowly, creating just enough friction where we are joined to keep spinning the pressure tighter and tighter inside. I whimper and beg, "Kayden, please..."

He releases one of my hands and reaches between us. His fingers press over my swollen clit. Pleasure bursts through me. Everything draws tight inside me before snapping loose. I'm crying out as another orgasm crashes through me in slow, intense waves. He surges into me so deeply that I can feel the force of my climax in my bones.

I'm gasping and trembling all over when I feel the heat of his release fill me as he thrusts inside me one last time. He cries my name and shudders over me.

On the heels of a breath, he rolls us over until I rest atop him. I feel as if I've crashed ashore after a storm. The pleasure is like a receding tide of slow, lapping waves through my body. We breathe together, and I can hear the thundering beat of his heart slowing where my head rests against his chest.

Eventually, I shift, sliding my palm onto his chest and lifting my head to rest my chin on the back of my hand. Kayden's fingers sift through my hair before his palm slides down my back. He opens his eyes to meet my gaze.

There's something pure and also carnal about the look in his eyes. He looks as entirely sated as I feel. I feel liquid, utterly relaxed in a way I never have before. His eyes hold mine, and it feels like a shimmer in the air around us.

"What now?" I ask.

His fingers trace idly down my back, and I love the subtle sensations that spin through me with every touch from him. "We're staying here for the week. I understand they call it a honeymoon on Earth. Here, we call it pleasure."

His lips curl in a slow smile, and even though I've just found more pleasure than I ever could've imagined, my belly does a little shimmy and a dance.

"A whole week?"

It's not that I don't understand the concept of a honeymoon. On Earth, only the wealthy can even contemplate a honeymoon. I had dreaded time alone with my ex.

Romance is scarce on Earth. It's grim there. Although my ex claimed I would enjoy life with him because I would get to live in the green zone, I hadn't looked forward to it, not even a little. I can't imagine what I will do for an entire week. I have worked twelve hours a day since I was fifteen. At least I had a job.

"Only the wealthy have honeymoons on Earth," I finally say, kicking those old memories to the curb.

Kayden's gaze sobers as he studies me. "This is your home now. Everyone can have a week to themselves if they want it."

I take a breath. An ever-present tension that I have carried inside me for most of my life—the stress and fear that marked my life on Earth—starts to ease. I swallow, and my eyes sting a little bit with tears.

Kayden lifts his head slightly, giving me a gentle, lingering kiss. When he draws away, he trails his knuckles along my cheekbone. "The bruising is almost gone," he says.

I nod wordlessly. "Tell me more about what happened," he says.

His tone is gentle, but a thread of steel is woven inside it. I know that if we were on Earth, he would protect me. Maybe it shouldn't matter, but it does. Warmth surrounds my heart.

"I don't know how much you know about life on Earth beyond the fact that we destroyed the environment over a century ago."

"We know that. Intergalactic travel has existed since before the inhabitants of Earth destroyed their own environment. Things were getting bad when they really pushed to move out. Since they've had little to trade or offer with other planets, it hasn't been easy."

"Of course not. Around that time, things got much worse for women. I don't know what it was like before that for women. It isn't discussed in our history books, but it's whispered about. Around the same time, a contingent of humans refused to believe the climate was getting worse because of our actions. They also clamped down on women's rights. The only thing that gives me comfort is knowing that most women disagree with it. I don't know what it's like in the green zone, where the wealthy live. Rumor has it they have enough food and resources for themselves. The factory I worked in provided things for them. For as long as I've been alive, I've heard that they're working on rejuvenating our environment." I shrug with one shoulder. "Anyway, so life isn't good for women. We have to have permission from men for anything, such as where we live and so on. My ex's family was wealthy, and he decided he wanted me. At first, I thought it would be a good idea. There aren't many good options for women. The opportunity to live in the green zone was enough to make me go for it even though I didn't like him. But then, he started getting violent and controlling. I realized I would rather never live in the green zone than be with someone like him." I gesture toward the fading bruise on my cheek. "The morning I saw the ad for mates here, he came to my apartment. He threw me against the wall and punched me. I kicked him in the balls and left."

Kayden's lips twitch at the corners although anger swirls in his gaze. "Good for you. I would've done a lot worse than that."

"I wouldn't want anyone to kill him," I interject.

"Oh, I wouldn't have done that. We don't believe in murder. I would've made his life fucking miserable."

"I don't live on Earth anymore, and I'm never going back," I say firmly.

"You never have to go back, and I will keep you safe here." His words are spoken like a vow. "We treat our women well here."

"What about what happened to Jane?" I can't help but ask.

"I'm sure you've heard the rumors about the town on the other side of our planet. A small contingent of men there, well, they think like the men on Earth, the very people on Earth who ended up destroying their own environment. They refuse to acknowledge that mating with others has strengthened us because it keeps us healthier. The small group has manipulated elections to hold power in that one town. The people don't support them because they hoard resources, even though there are plenty. They want to intervene in the royal line of succession," he explains.

"That's what Jane said," I chime in. "But why did they kidnap her?"

"We believe they hoped to keep her until she had her baby and use the heir for leverage. They miscalculated. Now, we know how dangerous they are. We've had battles and skirmishes with them over the centuries."

"Do they treat their women badly there?"

Kayden considers my question. "Women hold power in our society, so they know they have to be careful about that. They try to control who the women mate with. They don't want them to mate with humans from Earth or those from other planets. The women do what they want anyway because they know they are protected by everyone else. Kidnapping Jane angered everyone because she was a woman and pregnant. Our royal family is beloved. They have taken care of us for century upon century."

"Do you worry about your safety?"

Kayden is quiet for a few beats before he shrugs. "I don't want you to be afraid. I protect the royal family as my family always has. I don't worry that harm will come, but providing such protection comes with certain risks. Risks I carry gladly."

He must see the alarm in my eyes because he lifts a hand, palming my cheek and tracing his thumb across my bottom lip. "You needn't be afraid. My family has protected the royal family for centuries."

The anxiety spinning inside loosens as I stare into his golden gaze. I don't know how to explain it, but I feel safer with Kayden and on this planet than I have ever felt in my entire life. I take a quick breath. "I have faith you'll stay safe."

Kayden dips his head and brushes his lips over mine, sending sparks scattering through me. "I will, and I promise to keep you safe. You will always be under my protection."

Chapter Eleven
KAYDEN

My promises to Nadine ring like a bell inside. I have given my heart to her. I pledged my protection to her, and I keep those promises.

I ponder her question about our safety as well. I know we have this week for ourselves, but after that, I will once again be focused on planning how to manage the upheaval on our planet.

Blessedly, the distraction of Nadine and the power of our infinity pulse is so strong that I'm not preoccupied by anything else during this week. I wake the following morning with her warm and soft beside me. She is delectable and irresistible. I'm spooned behind her, my thick arousal nestled in the plump curves of her bottom.

I can already feel my arousal dripping from the tip of my shaft. Until her, I had never claimed a human woman before. I never thought I would care about being the only one to claim a woman. But Nadine is *mine*. I have already marked her, and that knowledge burns like a fiery coal inside me.

I slide my hand over her belly, imagining her round with our child. When she shifts and lets out a little sigh in her sleep, I feel another drop of my seed roll out and down my shaft. I bring my hand up to her breasts, teasing her nipples lightly until I feel the awareness in her body. Her nipples are tight already under my touch. I dip my head to breathe her in and dust a kiss along the side of her neck.

"Kayden," she whispers, her voice velvety soft from sleep.

"Good morning, love," I murmur into her neck, gratified when I feel goose bumps prickle her skin.

She presses her hips back, letting out a little hum.

"How did you sleep?" I ask as I smooth my hand over her belly.

"Good," she says.

"Are you sore?" I ask as my hand shifts downward to her mound.

"I don't know."

"Can I touch you?"

"Please," she whimpers.

When I slide my fingers down between her thighs and find her slick, I nearly come against her bottom. She is soaked with her arousal, her thighs wet with it. Her clit is plump and swollen. I rock my hips into the cleft of her bottom.

I shift, rolling onto my back and bringing her with me. Moments later, I can feel her curves pressed against me.

"Kayden," she gasps as I smooth a hand over her bottom and into her folds.

I move back slightly, and her knees fall to the sides of my hips as I bring her up with me. Another shimmy back, and I'm seated against the pillows with a lapful of Nadine.

I glance down. The underside of my cock is nestled against her slippery core. Instinctively, she rocks her hips back and forth, biting her lip as she lets out a little sigh of satisfaction.

"I need you inside me," she says between ragged gasps.

I look down. Her clit pokes out, pink and plump. She's so fucking sexy. Control isn't usually an issue for me, but I have to scramble for it. The sight of her so ready for me is nearly enough to bring me to release.

The mingling of her arousal with my pre-cum is so slick, it's almost as good as being inside her. "I'll go slow," I tell her.

I nudge her upward, gripping my thick cock and positioning it at her entrance. "Watch," I say.

She looks down with me as I grip her hips and slowly bring her down over my length. It takes all of my control to keep from coming in her tight core. My cock is sheathed in her pink channel, and she's clenching and warm.

I tease my fingers over her swollen nub, and she lets out these tiny whimpers.

"Do you want to come for me?" I ask.

She lifts her eyes to mine. "Please..."

I rock my hips gently. "Is this okay?" I slide my palm up her back, levering her forward slightly, creating more friction where we're joined. "I want you to come, just for me."

Her lips part as she pants. I rock slowly into her, deeper and deeper with each thrust upward. I can feel the slippery fusion. She begins to tremble, and I catch her cry with a kiss. She clamps around my cock, milking out my seed. I feel it running down my shaft and over my balls.

She relaxes against me, soft and warm in my arms. I rock up once more as another spurt of my release fills her. She's dripping with it. I feel this intense satisfaction beyond feeling sated. It's the knowledge that I have claimed her again, that she will be carrying our baby soon.

Long moments later, I reluctantly ease her off me. Her cheeks are pink when she looks up. "You will be carrying our baby by the end of this week," I tell her.

Chapter Twelve
NADINE

Before coming to this planet and meeting Kayden, I couldn't have imagined a week like this. It's all pleasure. Again and again, we tangle together. My body is sore but in a purely sated way.

Kayden takes such good care of me. The first few times, he brought a warm cloth afterward and cleaned me between my thighs. He asked if I felt okay. I feel so far beyond okay. My entire body feels made of pleasure, all for him.

It's the last night before the end of our week alone. We're in the kitchen, and I'm seated on the counter, wearing a loose dress and no panties. They just get in the way, so I don't bother with them.

He pushes my skirt up around my hips, and I can literally feel the heat of his gaze on my sex. "You're wet again," he teases lightly, lifting his golden gaze to mine.

My pussy clenches at the look in his eyes, dark and filled with love and need. "It's you," I whisper.

He tugs my hips to the edge of the counter. Just when I think he's going to bring his mouth to my sex, he straightens again, pulling the top of my dress down under my breasts. It's a stretchy dress, and my breasts plump up over it. He sucks one nipple into his mouth and then the other. The piercing pleasure arrows to the core of me when he sucks them hard before lifting his head.

I look down to see my nipples pink and wet from his mouth. He pushes my thighs farther apart, his eyes on mine as he lowers his head and brings his mouth to my sex, fucking me with his fingers and tongue.

I'm desperate, my hands scrambling to find purchase on the counter. Just when I'm about to find my release, Kayden straightens, a teasing glint in his eyes as he swiftly frees his cock. The tip of it is glistening.

"Do you want this inside you, sweetheart? Do you want to come all over me?"

I plead, "Hurry, Kayden..."

He spreads my folds with the fingers on one hand and fists his thick length with the other. "Watch me fill you, sweetheart," he says.

I look down, watching his cock disappear inside me. My little clit pokes out. I'm coming almost instantly when he teases his fingers over that swollen nub. Seconds later, I feel the heat of his release filling me. He thrusts deep and hard inside me. He draws his cock out, smearing the tip of it in the slippery mess of my pussy as more of his seed spurts over me and drips on the floor.

He holds my eyes the whole time. I feel owned by him, and it's all I want.

Chapter Thirteen
KAYDEN

The following week

"They're doing what?" I ask Asher.

My closest friend and prince of our people rolls his eyes. "They are trying to organize protests."

"What exactly are they protesting?" I ask dryly.

"They are protesting the matchmaking service. They think we need to wait."

"Wait for what? Over half the women on our planet died during the storm. We're talking about losing an entire generation because we don't have enough women to mate. We've mated with humans for centuries. We are originally descended from humans," I point out.

Our kind descended from human cowboys from the western United States and gardians from France long before the earth began to dry up. Intergalactic travel has existed for centuries. Our people have been traveling widely over the galaxy, and those from Earth also traveled. Those cowboys were well suited to our planet with the flying horse-like creatures we ride here. Their willingness to explore and their boldness fit well. All over the galaxy, aliens have mated with each other, so this is nothing unusual.

On the far side of our planet, a group of people in another town has been the source of unrest time and again. They continue to challenge our royalty succession. Their latest move was to kidnap our new princess, Jane. She is safe and has already given birth to the next heir.

"There's not much they can do," I point out the obvious. "We need mates, and we will keep mating with humans. It's nothing new except that we must search for more women. We need them."

Asher nods. "Of course. We will send a team over there to monitor the demonstrations. They can protest all they want, but we need to know their plans. I'm hoping you'll lead that now that you are married." Asher's eyes hold a teasing gleam. "Do you think Nadine is carrying your child?"

"Absolutely. She doubts me, though." The thought of her plump with our child makes my cock twitch.

"You told her human women become more fertile on our planet?" my friend prompts.

"Of course, but I think she'll have to experience it herself."

"How do you feel?" he asks.

"I didn't believe in the infinity pulse, but I do now. I know she is full with our baby. I told her we'll know soon. Can I wait to go until I know for certain?"

"Of course. I presume you'll need to plan as it is. I thought we could ride over tomorrow just for the day to scout out the situation. After that, you can select who will go with you for the team."

I nod, and as I move to leave, I feel Asher's palm curling over my shoulder. I turn back. "What is it?"

"I'm glad you found Nadine. More than that, I'm glad you're experiencing the infinity pulse. You deserve it, my friend."

I can't help the slow smile that stretches across my face. "I had my doubts about the infinity pulse, but it's worth it. I only hope I never lose her."

Asher's gaze sobers. "I know the feeling." After a pause, he adds, "I'll see you tomorrow. We'll leave at dawn."

I depart Asher's office. The mere mention of Nadine has a restlessness humming in my veins. After I leave the offices, I walk down to the café where she has started working.

Our planet is safe except for the challengers to the royal succession. They've been making a racket ever since the storm killed so many women a few years ago. They see it as an opportunity to rattle for change. Yet they are greedy and selfish and want to take rights away from women. Our people worship women, and the challengers don't like it. They don't understand that without women being treated with honor, we become weaker.

Our town is centered around the government and royal headquarters. The beautiful buildings have lush gardens surrounding them. For transportation, many simply walk although some use hovering vehicles to travel through town. We also have horses that fly. I usually walk.

Nadine has worked her new job for the past few days, and I aim straight for the small café. When I walk inside, it's busy, and the fresh scents of food and coffee assail me.

Trudy, the orc who owns this café, towers over Nadine where they stand behind the counter together. Nadine hasn't noticed me yet, and I pause to take her in. Her wavy honey-colored hair is twisted into a knot with loose tendrils dangling around her cheeks. She smiles at something Trudy says to her. My heart beats faster and faster, and my tail twitches.

She must sense my presence because she lifts her eyes to mine. It's as if a flame licks through the air between us. Before meeting her and experiencing the infinity pulse, I couldn't have imagined the depth of feeling she evokes inside. The emotion itself heightens the fierce physical attraction.

I want to order everyone to leave us, to bend her over the

counter and fill her until my arousal drips down her legs. I cling to my discipline and simply walk to the counter.

Trudy's sharp gaze bounces between me and Nadine. "Shall I let her take a break?" she teases.

Nadine's cheeks flush a deep shade of pink. My cock lengthens to the point of pain as my tail twitches again. "If she would like one," I say.

Nadine swallows, glancing between us. "Am I allowed a break?"

She has lived on Earth, a life where she was treated barely above a slave. The orc is aware of this and glances at Nadine. "On this planet, you're treated well and can take several breaks each day. Go with your mate. Come back in a half an hour."

Moments later, Nadine walks beside me on the street, her hand warm in mine. "Where are we going?" she asks.

"To my office," I tell her.

I'm in a hurry, and I'm walking too fast. With her so much smaller than me, I know she can barely keep up. She sounds breathless. I force myself to walk more slowly.

We rush through the entrance to the building, up the stairs, and down the hallway. I'm beyond impatient to get to my office and relieved no one delays us along the way. When we finally get inside, I kick the door shut behind us and lock it. I pull her swiftly across the office. Nadine is wearing a dress because she knows I love them.

We stop in front of my desk, and I palm her cheek, looking into her eyes as I rock my hips against her.

Her lips fall open. "Oh," she breathes.

"I need you," I rasp against her mouth before claiming her with a devouring kiss.

I love how she doesn't hesitate, and her tongue tangles with mine.

"Turn around to face my desk," I say.

She turns quickly. I reach down to drag her skirt up over her hips. Her bottom is flushed pink from her desire. "Bend over," I command.

She does exactly as I ask. I glance down to see her pink pussy wet and glistening. The insides of her thighs are smeared with her arousal. I tug my breeches open. My own arousal is already rolling down my cock. I press against her, forcing myself to wait for at least a moment.

"Are you ready for me?" I ask.

"Please, hurry," she says in her prim little voice with a wiggle of her bottom.

Gripping my length, I position myself, notching at her entrance before filling her in one deep thrust. It's fast. My release hits me like a bolt of lightning as soon as I hear her cry out, pushing her bottom back to me as she clenches around me. I look down to see my cum-covered cock sliding in and out as I keep filling her until we both come again. Cum drips down her thighs onto the floor.

I help her put her dress back in place and clean up. Just before we walk out of my office, her eyes lift to mine. "I love you, Kayden."

When I kiss her, I almost have to take her all over again.

Chapter Fourteen
NADINE

"That'll be five coins," I tell the customer.

She smiles at me, flicking her tail as she pays. "Here you are."

I happily plunk her five coins in the register while Trudy hands her the coffee she ordered. I love my job so much that I don't even know what to think. I'm so accustomed to work being pure drudgery. The experience of a reasonable schedule, a boss I actually like, and customers who are kind to me make a remarkable difference.

Our day stays busy with one customer after another. As we roll into the afternoon, Trudy glances over with a smile. "So what do you think?" she asks.

"About what?"

"All of it. Life on a new planet, marrying one of the bodyguards for the prince." Her eyes hold a teasing glint. "And your job," she adds.

I'm wiping down the counter. I experience a shock at the rush of emotion that arises with her question. Tears sting my eyes. I swallow through the tightness in my throat and try to breathe through the clenching in my chest. I buy myself a moment as I finish wiping the counter. When I look up at her, I instantly realize she understands.

Her gaze is warm and kind. "I love it," I tell her earnestly. "So much it makes me want to cry, but they're happy tears." I pause. "Sort of. What I left behind was awful."

Trudy places her big hands on my shoulders and squeezes gently. She towers over me, and I feel incredibly safe around her because I'm confident she could easily protect me from anyone. "My life was different from yours on Earth, but it wasn't good before I came here. I was a warrior. I suppose I still am. I was given no choice but to fight. My planet isn't peaceful."

"I'm glad you're here now," I say.

Her lips twist as her hands drop away from my shoulders. "You were a fighter too, right?" she prompts.

I don't talk much about my life on Earth. In addition to my job, I was a fighter there. As the environment got hotter, plants and animals began dying in droves. Teams of fighters fought other humans, the worst of them. My family had been designated to fight. It wasn't as bad as it had been for my parents' generation, but I still had to fight sometimes when marauders came into our towns. I hated every minute of it. It wasn't as if they selected fighters based on skill. Those assigned to fight came from the bottom of the social class ranks. Despite all that, I was scrappy.

My fighting spirit is probably what led me to walk away from my ex once and for all. Even though I hated that part of my past, I still told Kayden about it. I don't want to hide anything from him.

I look up at Trudy. "I was a fighter." I gather my thoughts. "Do you ever lose that?"

She tips her head to the side as she studies me. "I don't think so. That fighting spirit is a part of you. But you no longer have to fight for your life. You're safe."

Just then, the door to the café opens, and Princess Jane strides in with Melody. I've seen them both a few times since Kayden and I had our week alone. I break into a big smile. I'm so grateful Jane selected me to come here, and I'm hopeful Melody will find her mate soon.

"Hi!" I say when they stop in front of the counter.

Jane's smile is warm. "Hello. Tell me, how are you? How are you enjoying your job?" she asks.

"I love it!" I say, clasping my hands together in front of my chest.

Trudy laughs softly as she smiles among us. "She really does, and she's really good at making coffee."

"Speaking of, what can I get for you, Princess?" I ask.

Jane's cheeks flush pink. "You really don't have to call me princess."

"I want to," I insist. Although I know she doesn't expect me to stand on ceremony, it's fun.

I make them both coffee and glance toward Melody while I work. "How are you?"

Melody purses her lips together. "Nervous." She slides her eyes to Jane. "Princess Jane is having another dinner party. She wants us to meet our mates."

"Great plan. When is it?" I ask.

"I haven't scheduled it yet, but it will be soon," Jane says. "I promise you and Kayden will be invited."

"I can't wait!" I waggle my brows when I meet Melody's gaze again.

The camaraderie and kinship I feel with the women here from Earth is like nothing I ever experienced while living there. Even if you cared about people, everyone scrambled to stay alive and get by. If you had a chance for something better, people walked over each other to get there. Even though I've only been on Aphroditea for a matter of weeks, there's absolutely no doubt, especially among the women, we take care of each other here. You feel it, not just from the women from Earth, but all of them. The reverence and kindness feel almost too good to be true.

I chat with Princess Jane and Melody for a few more minutes

before more customers arrive. Jane promises to notify me of the next dinner party when they leave. When the café closes, Kayden arrives, telling me he wants me to ride with him. He's told me this is something I need to learn. I'm a little anxious, but he makes it all easy.

His horse is a beautiful shimmery green. I have a mount to match whose coat is a lighter shade of green. She is kind and gentle. Even though I'm nervous, I smile over at him once I'm riding her. "I feel like she's taking care of me."

His eyes glitter gold as he looks over at me. A now familiar heat suffuses me as I meet his gaze. "She is. They have always protected our people, and you are one of us."

That night, he tells me he'll travel to the other side of the planet tomorrow with Asher and some other men.

"Will you stay safe, please?" I ask.

Chapter Fifteen
KAYDEN

As we fly, my horse, Callister, is as steady as ever. He comes to a landing with the team riding with Asher and me. We stop on an elevated rise outside the town on the other side of the planet.

The town looks quiet. I glance at Asher. "What do you think?"

We collectively scan the area. I see evidence of an outpost just before I start to bring my gaze back toward the town. Some animals are tethered to posts, and the corner of a tent is visible behind some boulders in the distance at the base of a mountain. "Over there," I say quietly with a nudge of my chin. Asher follows my gaze.

"That must be where they're meeting," Hunter offers. He's a security team lead. "We know they're not meeting in town. The rumors about the protests indicate they are small. They're trying to prevent a new election and make noise about the trials for those arrested for the kidnapping of Princess Jane."

Asher's eyes narrow. "Let's avoid the protests for now. We'll do a regular tour of the towns around the planet to avoid speculation. When we come here, let's raid the outpost. We'll start the tour in a month or two." He brings his attention to me. "I'd like your team to scout the area next week. Let's confirm it isn't just some youth camping before we move ahead."

One week later, Nadine waits for me when I get home. Her eyes are bright, and her cheeks are pink.

"What is it?" I ask.

"I've missed my monthly," she says.

A surge of pride rises inside me, an almost primal sensation. Before I can even ask, she adds, "The doctor already confirmed I'm pregnant."

She smooths her hand over her belly, and I step close to give her a lingering kiss. When we break apart a moment later, I want her fiercely. My desire for her is ever-present, and the knowledge she is with my child increases its force. Yet she's as fragile as spun glass now. The sense of protectiveness that rushes through me is unlike anything I've experienced.

I cup her cheeks, looking deep into her eyes. "Soon, we'll be a family."

She smiles, her eyes bright with unshed tears. "I'm so glad you chose me," she whispers.

"As if there was any choice. The infinity pulse beats between us."

I'm relieved we've confirmed she's now carrying my child. I can go on my journey with this knowledge. It will make me fight harder if I have to fight.

Chapter Sixteen
KAYDEN

Experiencing the infinity pulse sharpens my focus while we are away. Although Nadine is on the other side of our planet, it feels as if a thread connects us through time and space. While I've always taken my duties as a bodyguard for the royal family seriously, my love for Nadine deepens my commitment. It's no longer just my people I'm protecting. I'm protecting my love, my bride.

Our team scouts the outpost. We confirm it's a staging area for the small group of rebels. According to our history, this is merely the latest wave. My father has always told me that no matter what you do, there will always be those who want power solely for the sake of power. Even when a planet is peaceful and contented, there will be those who will jostle and create problems because they enjoy chaos and thrive in its aftermath.

Our government is a democracy, and our royal family is part of that democracy. They lead us because of their lineage. Perhaps that's confusing to some, but it has worked for our people since the beginning. There are many elected officials, and the royal leadership is voted on annually.

Yet here we are again with the latest rebel uprising arguing that the royal succession should change. I snort when I see one of the signs. *We want to be royal too.*

"They don't even want to get rid of the royal family. They just want to be part of it." I roll my eyes when I glance at Asher, who has decided to accompany us on this trip.

Asher lets out a low chuckle. "I know."

Hunter releases a low whistle of alarm as I feel the motion of air around us. Whipping my head around, I realize they've used an invisible net to capture us.

Asher's horse rears up and strikes its sharp hooves forward into the air, slicing through the netting. The rest of us move into formation, protecting Asher as he escapes the capture. Five of our group of ten men break through and follow Asher. For the remaining five, including me, the net drapes too closely for us to escape.

One of the rebels approaches from behind an outcropping of rocks, staring at those of us left behind. "They won't even come to get you. The princess is free," he sneers.

I lift my arm, flinging a fiery electric spear through the air directly toward him. He cries out and falls to the ground when it strikes him in the shoulder. It doesn't appear that anyone else is nearby. The five of us are left to begin to carefully untangle from the netting.

Chapter Seventeen
NADINE

"What do you mean? Kayden is captured?" I ask.

I stare at the prince and princess as a sense of panic claws inside me. My throat hurts.

The prince dips his head, looking deeply into my eyes. "Nadine, we are returning this evening to rescue them. We've already sent scouts out to assess the situation. Don't worry, we will bring Kayden back to you."

The euphoria of the past few weeks that had been protecting me from all my old fears has burned to ashes inside. A sense of hopelessness and darkness closes around me. *What will happen if Kayden is not okay? Will I be sent back to Earth?*

Rising through the noisy panic is an overriding sense of love. I was at work at the café when Trudy notified me a messenger had called me to the royal offices. I had hurried over. I didn't know what to think, and now I'm in shock.

My hands tingle. There's a sharp knock on the door. Asher barks out, "Enter!"

The queen comes walking into the office. She's dressed in fitted garments and flanked by a group of women, all of whom look fierce and strong. "We are the best fighters," she says. "We will go."

"I'm a fighter. I'll go with you," I interject.

All eyes swing to me. I clear my throat. "I am. My family lineage is fighting. I wasn't given a choice, but I do it well—"

Jane cuts in, "Nadine, you can't do that. You're carrying a child."

"I can do this," I say, my words a vow. "I'm a strong fighter. I'll be safe."

The queen assesses me, her eyes narrowing. It feels as if she looks straight through me. "You must come. Your love for Kayden will protect us all."

The moments that follow are a rush. One of the women with the queen brings me down the hallway and outfits me in fitted gear. It appears to be heavy leather, except it feels light on my body. "A sword cannot cut through this," the woman tells me. "We are honored to have a human join us. We are stronger when we join."

Inside of a blink, I'm in something like a plane. It's not quite like the ship that brought us here from Earth, but it's similar. The small and lightweight aircraft zooms across the planet's surface until we hover over some mountains outside another town. I can see the buildings and streets from here.

The aircraft lowers to the ground, and I follow the women out. The queen looks at me. "I do not want you to fight alone. Do you understand me?"

"Yes, Your Highness." I dip my head in acknowledgment.

The prince and the king are also with us. I'm slightly startled by their presence, but it helps me understand why the people here are so loyal to this royal family. Even though they're royal and it's their lineage, they clearly care. I can feel their concern reverberating, especially Asher's fear on behalf of his closest friend.

A group assesses how to approach the outpost while I feel a burning sensation in my chest. It's the very sensation I feel whenever I'm close to Kayden.

I approach the queen. "Kayden is near. I can feel him," I tell her.

The queen lifts her chin, her smile subtle and proud. "You do. That is the infinity pulse. You can help us find him. Walk in a small circle and begin making it bigger. Wherever you feel the strongest burn is where we will go," she says.

Following her guidance, I begin to walk in a slow circle. A moment later, my chest burns so hot that it hurts. The burn fades as I move away, so I turn back and gesture in that direction. A small rise obscures a cluster of boulders at the base of the mountain nearby. The women fan out, following the queen's directions. The king and prince take a separate group, looping around to the other side of the mountain.

Within moments, the burning in my chest becomes even more powerful. Seconds later, we see the group of men. The queen holds her hand up, and we collectively freeze in place. I've lost sight of where the king's security team has gone, but I suddenly hear shouting as fighting breaks out nearby. A motley group of alien men comes spilling out from the boulders, and we are in the thick of a fight. It is quick and fierce. Wrestling with one of the men, I discover an advantage. I grab his tail and pull it between his legs before yanking him upward and flinging him to the ground. Moments later, I disarm him.

My heart pounds, and adrenaline rushes through me. I let out a cry when someone grabs me from behind. I recognize the sound of Kayden's voice nearby. I'm grappling with this large alien man, and I fear he'll overpower me. Suddenly, he is lifted away, and I hear a loud crack as he falls to the ground.

When I lift my eyes, Kayden is before me.

He steps close as the sound of fighting carries on around us. Most of the battle is over, except for a few remaining scuffles. He gives me a fierce kiss before spinning away and joining the prince as they subdue the remaining men hiding in the boulders.

Although the queen leads a fierce group of female fighters, I notice there isn't a single woman among the fighters from this town.

I've heard stories that this group of rebels wants to eliminate the worship of women on this planet. They want to take away our power, and here we are, beating them at their own game.

Any injuries are mostly minor. As I stand there with my breath heaving, the queen approaches. "Nadine." She dips her chin, and I feel compelled to bow, but she shakes her head. "You are a powerful fighter. After you have your child, you can join our warriors."

Kayden comes over, sliding his arm around my waist. She looks over at him. "You did well in protecting the prince, but you always do. Your bride is an impressive warrior. She will be one of us now."

Without another word, she turns and strides over to the king. Another team arrives to handle the capture of the men who held Kayden and the others. Meanwhile, Kayden swiftly moves his hands over my body as if checking to confirm I'm all in one piece. One palm lingers over the curve of my belly. "I'm proud of you."

"I wanted to fight for you," I say. "I hope you don't mind, but I'd like to join the warriors with the queen after our baby is born."

His golden gaze darkens. "I will worry, but you are strong, and I believe in you. I would never keep you from what you are meant to do. You are meant to fight. Together, we are stronger."

When he pulls me close into his embrace, I feel as if I've come home. I could be anywhere in the galaxy, but as long as I'm with Kayden, I'm at home in my heart. He kisses me deeply before lifting his head. "There is much for me to do before I can return to our town."

"I understand," I say.

"You will fly back with the queen and her team. I will stay here with the prince and return later."

Even though I don't want to part with him, I understand his duty. I know that he will be with me as soon as he can. "I love you. Stay safe, *please*," I whisper.

He kisses me once again, and I press my fingers to my lips to hold on to the sensation.

Chapter Eighteen
KAYDEN

Nadine stares at me, her eyes wide as she holds my gaze, worry and love flickering there. She fought to save me, sending a wave of emotion crashing through me. I can't focus on her at the moment, though. I must focus on security for now. The elite fighting team of women and the rest of the security detail secure the area. They arrest those who held us captive and attempted to capture the prince.

I find it difficult to release Nadine's hand. Her gaze keeps sweeping to me as if to make sure I'm okay. I reluctantly let go and get to work.

Too much later, when I finally get home, it feels like it's been forever when it's only been hours. Nadine orders me into the shower and joins me when I call her name.

When human women mate with our kind, their pregnancy progresses much faster than if they mate with a human. Nadine's belly is already round, and I love how she looks. After we are both clean and dry, I run my hands over her, lingering over the curve of her belly. I lift her onto the bathroom counter and push her knees apart.

"Did you miss me?" I ask as I lift my eyes to hers.

"So much," she gasps.

I drag my fingers through her slippery wet folds. My seed drips out of my cock as I lift it to her, smearing the pearly-white liquid all over her. "Do you want me inside you?"

"Please," she begs, spreading her legs open a little more.

I fill her in a swift thrust, and we look down together as my cock slides in and out of her clenching core.

Her thighs begin to tremble, and I pull her a little closer to the edge, being careful not to push too hard because she's carrying our child. I tease her swollen clit with my fingers, savoring the ragged sound of my name when she cries out. My release sizzles like lightning at the base of my spine before I pump her full of my seed. She may already be carrying my baby, but I love claiming her, and I always will.

Chapter Nineteen
NADINE

"You look beautiful tonight," Princess Jane says.

I feel beautiful. My rapidly progressing pregnancy means my belly is already round and plump. I feel deeply connected to the baby growing inside me and just as profoundly connected to Kayden.

It's been weeks since the skirmish on the other side of the planet, and he has doted on me since. When I think of how he literally worships my body on a daily basis, I flush.

I smile back at Jane. "Thank you." I take a breath. "Thank you for bringing me here." Emotion rises swiftly inside. Jane selecting me to come here has dramatically changed my life. I still marvel at it and will for the rest of my life.

"I'm so glad you're here," she answers, her hands resting on my shoulders and squeezing gently. "Now, let's hope Melody and Romi find their mates soon. We have more women to bring here too." She pauses as her hands fall away before tilting her head to the side. "I'm wondering if you could help as we bring more women here from Earth. I know the transition can be challenging. You've adjusted so well, and you've made friends through your job at the café. Maybe we could create something like a support group. A place where women can learn about the planet and perhaps feel more comfortable. I was a little overwhelmed at first, but I had the protection of Asher."

"I would love that!" I clasp my hands together in front of my chest. "Let me know what I can do. As you know, I'll be giving birth soon, but I'm happy to do anything you need me to do."

Jane's smile is warm. "Have your baby. We can start doing the groups after that. I'm planning to travel to Earth every other month. At first, I thought I would go to Earth almost every week, but that isn't practical because I have a baby. Also, while we need women to mate here, we need to pace it to handle the weddings and so on. Do you think that's manageable?"

"Of course! That sounds perfect. I'll start thinking about where we can meet and what we can do."

We're at a dinner at the royal hall hosted by the prince and princess. Jane had originally considered hosting dinner at her home but decided she wanted to be able to host a large group.

It's so beautiful here. I've been to Kayden's office a number of times now and blush whenever I think of it. He usually wants to bend me over his desk. Of course, I want him to do that. I digress...

The white high-rise is beautiful, with windows everywhere. It's a circular shape with a courtyard in the center. They host dinners and meetings with other planetary emissaries in the large hall here. Tonight, men are milling about with the two groups of women who've come from Earth. Aside from those of us who landed with the first group, another group of four has arrived.

I approach Melody and Romi. They smile at me. "You look so good," Melody says.

She stops by the café often to see me. She has taken a job at a small flower shop across the street, so I see her frequently. She loves her job but is impatient to meet her mate.

"Marriage seems to be agreeing with you, along with pregnancy," she adds with a grin.

I smooth my hand over my belly. "They are both agreeing with me. Tonight, I'm hoping you'll meet someone for you."

Melody looks nervous. "I do too. And, honestly, I don't care whether I experience the infinity pulse. Because of how women are protected here, it will be okay no matter what."

"It will," I agree, "but I want you to experience the infinity pulse. It's amazing."

I know Kayden is approaching because I feel the slight burn in my chest. He stops beside me, sliding his arm around my waist.

Melody smiles over at him. "Hi, Kayden. I was just telling Nadine how beautiful she looks tonight. Her pregnancy and marriage seem to be suiting her well."

Kayden's palm slides onto my hip and squeezes. "She always looks beautiful, and I sure hope marriage and pregnancy suit her."

I roll my eyes as I look up at him, a sense of warm affection spinning around my heart. "You know they do," I tease lightly.

Just then, another man approaches, his tail twitching as he approaches us. Kayden catches his eyes. "Hello, Hunter."

Kayden gestures toward me. "This is my bride, Nadine, and this is Melody. She also came from Earth." Kayden glances between Nadine and me. "Hunter is part of the security for the governmental offices here. He travels with our planetary emissary team when needed."

Hunter is equal in height to Kayden, his eyes a darker shade of gold, almost caramel brown. When his eyes lock with Melody's, I know instantly they will mate. The infinity pulse is tangible in the air between them. I recognize the startled look in Melody's eyes. It's an overwhelming sensation.

Kayden squeezes my hip again, leaning down to whisper, "Let's leave them."

Chapter Twenty
KAYDEN

When Nadine sits up in the darkness, I immediately jolt awake.

"What is it?" I ask.

"The baby is coming," she says.

She might as well have struck me with a bolt of lightning. I sit up swiftly. "Let's go!"

"Kayden, we don't have to rush. The doctor told us when I felt my first contractions, it would still be hours before the baby came."

Her tone is soothing, and she doesn't even sound worried. Meanwhile, I'm barely listening to her as I fling on my clothes and tap my communicator for the medical team.

Nadine is full with our child. It's a little girl, and we have chosen a name. Delia, after my mother.

Nadine has been calm throughout her pregnancy. Meanwhile, according to her, I have started to drive her crazy over the past few weeks. And not in a good way.

She stands and wraps herself in a loose, flowing robe.

When my communicator beeps, indicating the medical team is here, it's all I can do not to fling my wife over my shoulder and cart her out. The only reason I don't is because it might harm the baby. I wrap an arm around her waist, walking beside her as she moves toward the front of our house. "Go get my bag, please," she tells me.

I'm usually a man in control, but I'm not now. I've forgotten we have a bag ready for her stay at the birthing center. I race to the closet off the entryway and fetch it. By the time I get back to the door, Nadine sits in a small hovering craft we use for medical transport in the main part of town. It feels as if nothing can happen fast enough for me as I bark out orders while the medical team goes about their business quickly and efficiently.

Just before we arrive at the medical center, Nadine reaches over and curls her hand into mine. Her touch soothes me instantly.

"I'm safe. I'm having our baby, and it will be okay," she says softly.

I look into her eyes, and the infinity pulse burns in my chest. I take a slow breath before leaning forward to give her a lingering kiss. "I'll calm down when you have our baby, and you are both healthy and safe."

The next few hours are a blur. I know logically that Nadine is in the best hands. Our planet is renowned for its medical care. Different aliens from all over the galaxy travel here specifically to receive our medical care. Yet I'm a wreck. My emotions are a jumble and all tangled up inside. While I'm with Nadine, it feels as if every moment is hazed with my anxiety.

Finally, I hear the cry of our baby girl. One of the nurses stops beside me. "Mama and baby are safe and well," she says.

Tears roll down my cheeks. She guides me over to Nadine's side, where they're placing our little baby girl in her arms. When humans mate with us, sometimes our offspring have tails, but not always. In this case, our baby girl has a sparkly pink tail. When Nadine holds her close, her tail curls around her hips.

For the first time in weeks, I can relax. The infinity pulse beats between us, encircling our baby in protection.

Nadine looks up, her face flushed and her smile tired. "I told you it would be okay," she whispers.

It is *so* much more than that. I brush her damp hair away from her face and lean forward to dust a kiss on her forehead. "I love you," I tell her.

EPILOGUE

Melody

I stare up at this alien cowboy, feeling breathless. Some qualities about the men on this planet feel so human. I'm aware they descended centuries ago from humans and have mated with us, but it's still a strange feeling. The man's caramel eyes study me, and I don't know what to think of this feeling inside. I feel liquid and hot all over.

"Melody," he says.

"Yes?"

"That's a lovely name." He takes a step closer, and I feel a visceral pull in my chest, almost as if a cord connects us and draws tighter the closer he gets.

Heat rises in my cheeks, and my pulse skitters wildly out of control, racing at a breakneck pace.

"Thank you," I whisper breathlessly, a little disconcerted. I swallow and scramble for my composure. "I forgot your name."

"Hunter." He takes another step closer, reaching for one of my hands.

I don't hesitate or pull away, which is unusual because I'm terrified of men.

Ever since I was selected to come to this planet to mate with an alien space cowboy, I have been so relieved to escape the desolate, lonely life I'd been leading on Earth. I've been here almost two months now and have been starting to despair of ever meeting a mate.

Jane, the princess, keeps telling me that it takes time. It's not that I doubt her, but Nadine found a mate before we even left the planet. I tell myself it's okay, that I don't need to experience the mythical infinity pulse that's supposed to exist here.

With Hunter near, it feels like my body is lit up with sparks, and I wonder if it's the infinity pulse. I've never even kissed a man or touched a man beyond being beaten by my own father and the other men in my family. I have no idea what to expect. Simply not being abused is more than enough for me.

But this feeling is overwhelming. This pleasurable, unfamiliar sensation between my thighs is making me slick and needy.

Hunter's hand is warm, his grip strong and firm. He lifts my hand and turns it over. He dips his head and drops a kiss in the center of my palm. It's a shock to my system, a sizzling sensation rippling throughout my body.

I inhale sharply. He takes another step closer. It feels like we have an electrical force field around us, snapping and crackling. My knees feel liquid, and that strange sensation between my thighs becomes more powerful. It feels empty—as if I need something there—and I know Hunter can fulfill that.

I lick my lips. "What's happening?"

He takes another step closer. When he brushes against me, I feel a thick, hard length swelling against me. "You will be my mate," he says with slow deliberation, his voice low and gruff. "I will talk to the prince tonight, and we will marry in a week."

Thank you for reading Kayden & Nadine's story - I hope you loved it!

If you'd like a glimpse from their future, you can join my newsletter to receive an exclusive scene.

Sign up here: https://BookHip.com/JVBGVQZ

. . .

Up next in the Match Made in Space Series is Mate for the Space Cowboy. When Melody signs up to move to a new planet, she just wants to be safe. She doesn't expect to fall for the broodiest of the broody alien cowboys. Buckle up for more space cowboy spice!

One-click to pre-order: Mate for the Space Cowboy - due out March 2025!

Sign up for my newsletter, so you can receive information about upcoming new releases & deals: https://phoebebelle.com/

ABOUT THE AUTHOR

Phoebe Belle lives on Earth. She loves escaping into happily-ever-afters, her family - human, canine and maybe even alien (not willing to rule that out because you never know!) - coffee and cooking.

https://phoebebelle.com/

facebook.com/phoebebellegalaxyromance
instagram.com/phoebebellegalaxyromance